The walls started to shake. The room tilted, settled again. I clutched at the arms of the chair. *Earthquake?*

And then . . . I couldn't believe what I was seeing. The ceiling was lifting right off, the way you'd lift a lid off a box, and the space above was almost filled by a huge head, big as a dinosaur's. A woman's face.

Mrs. Shepherd!

OTHER NOVELS BY EVE BUNTING

EVE BUNTING

THE LAMBKINS

Illustrations by Jonathan Keegan

JOANNA COTLER BOOKS
HarperTrophy®
An Imprint of HarperCollins*Publishers*

HarperTrophy® is a registered trademark
of HarperCollins Publishers.

The Lambkins
Copyright © 2005 by Edward D. Bunting and Anne E. Bunting,
Trustees of the Edward D. Bunting and Anne E. Bunting Family Trust
Illustrations copyright © 2005 by Jonathan Keegan
Library of Congress Cataloging-in-Publication Data
Bunting, Eve.
    The Lambkins / by Eve Bunting.— 1st ed.
      p.   cm.
    Summary: After being kidnapped by the lonely widow of a brilliant
geneticist, Kyle finds himself shrunk to doll-size and living with three other
children in a dollhouse from which there seems to be no escape.
    ISBN-10: 0-06-059908-1 (pbk.) — ISBN-13: 978-0-06-059908-9 (pbk.)
    [1. Genetic engineering—Fiction. 2. Kidnapping—Fiction. 3. Dollhouses—
Fiction.] I. Title.
PZ7.B91527Lam 2005   2004026184
[Fic]—dc22   CIP
                                                                        AC
Typography by Neil Swaab

First Harper Trophy edition, 2006

To Edward
—E.B.

THE LAMBKINS

CHAPTER 1

It was eight-thirty on a warm California night when the woman kidnapped me.

I was on my bike, coming home from my art class at the Marengo Gallery when I saw her. I was in a great mood. The gallery had had a display of students' work in the window and a collector had bought mine. Only mine! Richard, our teacher, had thumped my shoulder and beamed at me. "A hundred bucks! Not bad for a kid in ninth grade."

"Easy with the kid stuff," I'd growled. But I was stoked. Really stoked. I couldn't wait to tell Mom as soon as she came home from work. A hundred bucks!

That's what I was thinking about when I saw the woman.

She was standing by her car at the side of Anney's Road. The lid of the trunk was raised, and it wasn't hard to see she was in trouble. She looked nervous. No wonder. Anney's Road is dark and quiet.

I always came this way after my Tuesday and Thursday night classes because there's hardly any traffic and no speed bumps. I could cruise along, my bike light making a pool of yellow on the pavement, sometimes a possum or a skunk skittering across in front of me. The houses on one side of the road are big, set back behind high gates and walls. I never saw anybody going out of them or going in. On the other side is this open field area, not built up or anything. It's nice. You can almost imagine you're in the country. Anney's Road cut off ten minutes' riding time for me. But sometimes, like when there's wind moaning in the trees, it's scary, and then I push hard and buzz through, fast as I can.

I almost didn't stop when I saw her. I'm fourteen years old and a guy, but even so I know better than to stop for a stranger at night.

But this was a woman, about my mom's age, all

alone. I couldn't just zip on past and leave her there. Didn't she have a cell phone? I mean, everybody has a cell phone. Why didn't she use that to get help if she needed it?

I slowed and called out, "What's wrong?" At the same time I was checking to make sure she *was* alone and that there wasn't somebody else in the car or hanging around just to jump on me or whatever. I've heard about this kind of thing. No use taking chances.

She was alone.

I stopped, leaning with one foot on the pavement.

"I've got a flat tire," she said. "Thank goodness you came by. I can change it okay. But"—she spread her hands—"would you believe I can't get the spare and the jack out of the trunk? If you could just help me do that . . ."

Of course I'd end up having to change the tire for her. What was I going to do? Let her do it by herself? Man! I was already wishing I'd coasted on by. Now I was stuck.

Her headlights were off, but in my bike light I could see her pretty well.

She was wearing jeans and a heavy white sweater, and as she walked toward me I saw that her hair was that funny, artificial red that I guess some women think is pretty. Her smile was nice, though. I had this odd feeling that I'd seen her somewhere before. That too-red hair was ringing a bell.

"I was just thinking of hiking to the nearest gas station." She pointed into the trunk. "I'm afraid the spare and the jack are both under the floor section, all the way at the back."

"Okay," I said. "No problem." I hesitated. "Do you have triple A, by any chance? They'd change the tire for you. They changed a tire once for my mom when I wasn't around. Do you have a cell? You could call."

"I don't have a cell," she said. "How stupid can I get?"

Of course, even if she had a phone and called them I'd still have to hang with her till they came, so it made sense just to change the tire myself and get it over with.

I got off my bike and laid it on the grass at the side of the road, wedged far enough out of the way in case a car did happen to come by, then shrugged out of my backpack.

About a million crickets were singing in the fields that bordered the road. The little breeze carried the scent of jasmine, the kind we have in our backyard. I turned to smile at her, then leaned far into the trunk. It was dark and empty. My fingers searched for the crack that would let me lift up the carpeting and get at the spare-tire well, and that was when I felt a sting, right on my butt. It was a sharp sting that pierced the fabric of my cargo pants. "What the heck!" I yelped. I jerked back, but I was off balance and she pushed me. "Wait a sec—" I began, and then it seemed my mouth wouldn't work and my words wouldn't come. "Let me . . ." I mumbled and I tried to turn my head, but it wouldn't turn.

The trunk was half closed on me now, the metal biting into my thighs, and she was talking softly. At least I thought she was talking, saying, "Just relax," over and over. Vaguely I felt the trunk lid opening all the way and my legs being crumpled into the dark space along with the rest of me. And that was all.

CHAPTER 2

I was in a room, lying on a rug. A skinny African-American girl, who looked about my age, seemed to float above me. I closed my eyes, and when I opened them again I saw that she was kneeling beside me, holding a basin close to my face. I smelled vomit.

"Are you going to throw up some more, or are you finished?" she asked.

I stared at her. "Who . . . ?" And then I began to retch, shuddering and jerking and coughing into the plastic basin.

There was an older Asian guy watching me, too, standing behind the girl, and a little kid sitting cross-legged on the floor. A small dog lay panting beside her.

"Pe-ew!" the kid said, and held her nose.

I collapsed back on the rug.

"Here." The guy handed me a tissue, and I wiped my mouth. My stomach heaved.

"I think there's more," I whispered, and there was. When I was finished, he gave me another tissue.

"Think it's safe to empty this now?" the girl asked. She had the darkest eyes.

I tried to nod, and the top of my head seemed to lift off the rest of me. "Ow." I raised my heavy, heavy hand to feel if my scalp was still there and got a look at what was in the basin. It wasn't pretty.

"Sorry," I whispered.

She shrugged. "Don't worry about it. We've all gone through it. Mac, will you empty this for me?"

"Sure." The guy looked down at me. "Was it the old flat-tire trick with you?"

"I guess," I said. "What's going on? Where am I? Who are you?"

The little kid came cautiously across to look at me. She was wearing pink tights and a pink skirt, ragged at the hem, as if it had been cut down. Her T-shirt had a pink bear on the front.

"She did the old balloon trick on me, didn't she, Mac?"

7

The guy put his arm around her shoulders. From down here he looked enormously tall, towering over me. "She sure did, LuluBelle," he said gently.

"But we're going to get away real soon, right?" she asked, staring up at him. His face was wide with a wide mouth, his hair black as licorice.

He shrugged. "Got to go empty this," he said. "I'll be back."

Who were these people? Was I dreaming? I closed my eyes and opened them again, but they were all still there, except the older guy, who hadn't come back.

"Do you think you can get up now?" the girl asked. "I know it takes a bit of time. And you'll be dizzy. Lulu was the worst. She's so small the dose was probably too much for her. For a while Mac and I were really scared. John, too."

"John was nice," Lulu said. "I cried a lot when he went, didn't I, Tanya?"

"You sure did," Tanya said

I levered myself onto one elbow. The room swam around me.

I stood, swaying, and the girl came to my side and helped me into a chair. It was an easy chair, velvet or something. A white lamp with a pleated shade was on the table beside it. The dog jumped up on my lap and the little girl scolded, "Just wait, Pippy. He's still sick."

"It's all right." I liked the warmth of the dog, the weight of him across my knees. He felt normal, and nothing else did. Fear was suddenly thick in my throat. Something bad was going on here. Something terrifying.

"What's your name?" Lulu asked.

"Kyle," I said. "Kyle Wilson."

The girl nodded. "I didn't even remember my name at first. I think remembering is probably a good sign. I'm Tanya," she added.

"Tanya," I repeated. "Well, thanks for catching everything in that basin."

She smiled down at me. "That's okay."

She was Tanya. The tall guy who'd left was Mac. The little girl in pink was Lulu and the dog was Pippy. But who were they?

I looked around the room, careful not to move my eyes too fast. My head didn't feel too securely attached to the rest of me.

We were in a living room. It had a dark wooden floor with a cheerful blue-and-red tufty rug that might have been handmade. My aunt Ruth made rugs like that, but not so big. Three of the walls were painted a pretty shade of soft yellow, one a deep, rich blue. There was a blue couch, three chairs, a bookcase that held no books, and a dark wood table with carved legs. The six high-backed chairs had red-and-blue tapestry on the seats. There was something missing, though. It took me a few minutes to realize what it was. There were no windows, just those four blank walls. And there was only one door, which seemed to lead into an inside corridor.

They were watching me. I didn't want them to see how freaked out I was.

I rubbed Pippy's ears, and he squiggled happily against me.

"What's all this about?" I asked. "Where's the woman who brought me here? What does she want? She stuck a needle—"

"She's Mrs. Shepherd," Lulu said, and immediately put her thumb in her mouth.

"She can't come in here," Tanya added.

Lulu took her thumb from her mouth. "That's because we're Lambkins and she's not," she told me. "But you can be in here. Because now you're a Lambkin, too."

CHAPTER 3

Tanya brought me a

glass of water, and I took a few sips before I spoke. My hand shook, and I spilled water down my shirt. There were so many questions. Pippy jumped off my lap and ran to Lulu, who picked him up.

"What kind of a dog is he?" Of all the things I could have asked, this had to be the simplest.

"He's a *she*. And she's a fox terrier. She's a champion. Mrs. Shepherd says she can have a CH for champion in front of her name if she wants. Then she'd be CH Pippy."

I put down the glass. "Can one of you tell me what's going on?" I asked. "Are we locked in here . . . did this woman . . ." I paused. "Did she kidnap all of you . . ." I paused before I got the last word out. "Too?" I couldn't believe how weird that sounded.

"She also took John," Tanya said. "I guess you're a replacement for him. We figured she'd get someone. She likes four."

"Replacement?"

"We have four bedrooms," she added, as if that explained everything. "We also figured you'd be a white boy, same as John. The Shepherd likes a nice mixture. She has a reason for everything. She says she'd never buy a box of chocolates all the same flavor."

I stood up, holding on to the arms of the chair. "I'm not staying here. She has to be nuts. I'm— Where's the door?"

I staggered across the room, across the carpet with its dizzying colors. I fell. Tried to get up. Fell again. I stayed down. Not right yet.

"Easy. Easy." Mac must have finally come back. It looked like he had two faces now. "There is no door." His voice was flat and definite.

I could feel tears coming, and I swallowed them down. "But she can't—"

"She can," Tanya said.

I took a deep breath, pulled my knees to my chest, and looked up at them. Thank goodness they each had only one face now. Fear rumbled around in my stomach. Maybe I was going to throw up again. I tried hard to concentrate.

Mac, Asian. Tanya, black. Lulu?

"Lulu's Latina," Tanya said as if reading my mind. "Her name is really Lupe. Lupe Sanchez."

Lulu nodded. "I like Lulu for a name. It's cute."

"What did you mean, about being Lambkins? What's a Lambkin?" I had to be calm. I had to figure this out.

Mac shrugged. "That's what she calls us. Mrs. Shepherd and her Lambkins."

Tanya rolled her eyes.

"Does she hurt you? Us?" I asked. My words were weak and wobbly. I'd seen news reports of kids who'd been kidnapped and—

"Oh, no! Mrs. Shepherd would never hurt us. Mrs. Shepherd loves us." Lulu glanced nervously around the room and whispered. "I love her a little bit. But I'm scared of her, too. She's so *big*."

I didn't remember the woman who'd pushed me into the trunk being big. "Are you talking about the woman with the bright red hair?" I asked.

Lulu nodded twice. "It's really red. My mama has nice hair. And she's ordinary size." Her bottom lip quivered. "I want to go home."

"Shh, baby. Shh!" Tanya stroked Lulu's cheek. "You love us, don't you? Mac and me?"

"Yes. And I love Pippy, too."

My mind darted around, trying to make sense out of this.

"What time is it?" I asked Tanya.

She looked at her watch. "It's ten after six."

"What?" I stood, and this time I stayed up. Back to the chair. Needed to sit. "What day?"

"Wednesday," Mac answered.

"But—but it was Tuesday when she took me."

"I know. It seems to take about a day."

"For what? For your head to come back? But . . . what does she want?"

"Ah." Mac raised his eyebrows. "That's the million-dollar question right there. And there are maybe a million answers."

There was a pillow on the chair. It had HOME SWEET HOME needlepointed on it. I put it in my lap to fill the cooling place where Pippy had lain, and gripped it tight.

"Mrs. Shepherd says we are to be her children because she never had any," Lulu said. "She says all she ever wanted in the whole world was to have children." She kissed the top of Pippy's head. "And to have a dog. But she wasn't allowed. She says every family should have a dog. And we're a family. But we don't like it here."

"We hate it," Tanya said. "At least some of us do." She shot a glare at Mac, who looked away.

I strained to catch ahold of this. "But . . . wait a minute, we're not children. I mean, Lulu is . . ." I was looking from Mac to Tanya. "But the rest of us aren't."

"We are, to her." Mac sat down cross-legged on the rug, and a memory stirred.

"Hey!" I said. "I know who you are. You're McNamara Chang! You're the Valley High baseball pitcher. Big star. You disappeared. They beat the bushes for you! Everyone was talking about it. Even the *Times* had the headlines down here." The details were coming back now. The bold, black print. MCNAMARA CHANG DISAPPEARS. STAR PITCHER MISSING SINCE YESTERDAY.

15

"You were jogging," I said slowly. "You took your car up to some mountain trail. They found the car."

"They didn't find me," Mac said. "Mrs. Shepherd had a flat tire that evening, too."

My heart was punching against my chest. "But that was months ago!"

"I know," Mac said.

Tanya folded herself down across from him on the rug.

"Nine months. I've been here seven. Lulu four."

"And Pippy four, too," Lulu added. "We have it all marked on our calendar."

I was shivering, and the dizziness was coming back.

"I don't get it—" I began, but Tanya put her fingers to her lips. "Shh! I hear her coming. She's going to take you up for dinner."

"What?"

There was a scrabbling noise over our heads, and we all looked up at the ceiling. *There must be an attic*, I thought.

Pippy began to bark.

Lulu's thumb was back in her mouth.

16

The walls started to shake. The room tilted, settled again. I clutched at the arms of the chair. *Earthquake?*

And then . . . I couldn't believe what I was seeing. The ceiling was lifting right off, the way you'd lift a lid off a box, and the space above was almost filled by a huge head, big as a dinosaur's. A woman's face. The hair red as fire, her skin etched with crevices that you could fall into, the pores in her skin big as potholes. I could see into the twin black caverns that were her nostrils. Her earrings were gold hoops big enough to swing in. The smell of jasmine was overpowering.

Mrs. Shepherd! But she'd changed into a giantess, fearsome, grotesque.

"Lambkins," she said. "You've all met your new brother? Kyle Wilson?"

No one answered. My insides felt loose. I squeezed my arms tight against my stomach to stop them from falling out. And then, this gigantic hand came down to hover over me.

I crouched back in the chair and held the HOME SWEET HOME cushion in front of my face, trying to hide. Was I still drugged out? Was I going crazy?

The hand came closer. The gloved fingers fastened around me, and I was lifted like a doll through the place where the ceiling had been and held just inches from Mrs. Shepherd's huge, staring eyes.

"Hello, my new little Lambkin," she boomed. "Come to Mama!"

CHAPTER 1

I was lifted, up, up, up.

It was like being on some crazy ride in an amusement park, except that I wasn't buckled in. Her grip was tight around my waist as I whooshed high in the air. I grasped the bulk of her gloved thumb. What was she doing now? Oh, no! She had wedged me under her arm. I felt the roughness of her sweater, heard her grunt a little, the sound like thunder against me. I smelled that jasmine smell again. My face was wedged against the swell of her breast. She was putting the flat roof back on, lifting it like it weighed nothing, clicking giant metal clips all around it to keep it in place.

"There," she said. "All safe and sound."

With another *whish* of air against me, I was back in her giant hand. We were going up steps, so high and wide I would have needed a ladder to get from one to the next. My insides bounced each time she stepped up. Looking down, I could see her feet in red shoes with skinny heels. I twisted my head. Stucco walls, flaking a little, plaster crumbs stuck on them, each one the size of a snowball.

We reached the top.

She was walking, holding me in her hand close to her side, her arm swinging. I was back in the amusement park, on those chairs that sway back and forth like pendulums. My stomach heaved and I threw up. It wasn't much; there was just about nothing left in me that hadn't come up already. I saw the small trail of vomit below me. She didn't seem to notice at first, but when she did, all she said was "Oops! Sorry, Kyle," and held me upright in her fist.

"Here we are," she said. "I hope the ride wasn't too uncomfortable."

She set me on my feet on a rug.

"Would you mind just taking off your shoes before I seat you?" she asked. "They make such messy marks on my table."

I pulled off my shoes, which wasn't hard to do. There were no laces in them anymore.

"Thank you."

She lifted me up onto a wide, polished surface. I staggered uncertainly and unexpectedly sat down, flat on my rear. I was on a huge table. There was a plastic bowl filled with daisies in the center, each one taller than I was. I stood up. Music was coming from somewhere. It was *Coltrane Plays the Blues*. I knew the song. It's my mother's CD, but I like to listen to jazz while I paint in the gallery. Had Mrs. Shepherd gotten it somehow?

My brain fumbled with the thought, made no sense from it. I made myself look around. At one end of the table was a huge, green, fringed place mat, and beside me, on top of the mammoth table, was another table, smaller, made of dark wood. It was just like the giant one. On it was a smaller place mat, also fringed and green. Both tables were set for dinner with white plates and bowls, painted with roses. The smaller dishes were plastic. There was a plastic glass, a plastic knife and fork and spoon. The other plate was as big as a serving tray. I could have taken a bath in the water glass. She pointed to a chair that was drawn up to the smaller table. It looked as if I would actually be sitting there.

"Please have a seat, Kyle," she said.

I did. My nervous legs were happy to sit down.

She took off the leather glove and set it by her place, then leaned toward me. "Now I'm going to have to do something rather unpleasant and I hope you'll forgive me. I'm afraid it rather destroys the ambience of our first nice meal together, but I'm afraid it's necessary." She had something in her hand. At first glance I thought it was a whip, and I felt my skin crawl. But it wasn't.

"I'm going to have to put this leash on you and attach you to the leg of your table," she said, and bent over. I felt the whiplike thong curl around my ankle. She straightened again, her giant face flushed. "You see, once, when I was having a pleasant dinner conversation with John, he decided he wanted to leave me. He almost succeeded. Now I feel I have to take this rather disagreeable action."

"Is John all right?" My throat felt like sandpaper.

Mrs. Shepherd rubbed her forehead. "Unfortunately not. There was this horrible . . . accident. It almost broke my heart. I'm sorry that you didn't have a chance to meet him. I miss John a lot. He was

22

a good conversationalist, and I like that. But then"—
she spread her hands—"if he had still been here,
you wouldn't. I don't like the house to be too crowded.
When I was young, my home was horribly congested.
I longed for my own room." She gazed into space. "I
do miss John, though. He played a good game of
chess. He and I had quite a rivalry going, even
though the chess pieces weren't easy for him to
manipulate." She looked at me closely, the big eyes
considering. "I didn't come across anything in my
research that told me you play chess?" It was a
question.

I whispered, "No." I was mesmerized by those
eyes, each one as big as an alarm clock. I almost
thought I could hear them ticking. John Coltrane
was playing "Blues to Elvin" now. Everything was so
bizarre that I kept wondering if I was having one of
those terrifying nightmares that seem so real. She'd
been stalking me, checking up on me, "researching
me" before she took me. But why?

"Well!" Mrs. Shepherd smiled, and a gold tooth
glittered far back. A golden tombstone. "I might be
able to teach you. McNamara could be good, but he
resists spending the time. I understand. He's so
involved."

"What's he involved in?" I took a sip of my water, and the glass rattled against my teeth.

"Oh, his passion," she said vaguely. "But I can't complain. After all, that's one of the reasons I took him. Then of course there's Tanya. But she's so angry with me that all she does is stand in front of the chessboard and sulk. She's actually quite rude."

My brain had gone numb. All these riddles.

She smiled again, and I got the flash of the tombstone tooth. "Well, let's not talk any more about unhappy things. Are you comfortable? I didn't fasten the leash too tightly, I hope?"

I shook my head, which was a mistake. It wasn't ready to be shaken yet. I made myself look at her, at her huge, smiling face, her big clock eyes. *Ticktock, ticktock.*

"Why—why did you kidnap me?" I asked. "I don't get it."

"I didn't kidnap you! What a silly thought! Let's eat. I just fixed a nice meaty bouillon for you. None of my Lambkins has an appetite the first time we have dinner together."

She took our two bowls and went across to a buffet table. While her back was turned, I stared around the room. The chairs that ringed the table had high red-and-blue tapestry backs, just like the ones in the room I'd wakened in. Except that these were chairs big enough for a giant, like her. There was an identical hooked red-and-blue rug. Everything was the same, except huge and . . . in here there were windows hung with long blue velvet drapes. In one corner was a low stand that held a chess set, and close beside it, on the floor, was a huge black music case, the kind that might hold a double bass.

I looked back at the buffet table. There was a gigantic tureen, a platter of bread, and something else, something that made my flesh crawl again. A butterfly net! It was big enough to stop a charging buffalo. I didn't even have to think about it. I knew what it was for. Had that net trapped John as he tried to run for freedom? Had she lifted him out, wriggling and squirming? And then he'd had the "accident"? I'd noticed the way she'd paused before she said that word. I squeezed myself tight in the chair.

She was bringing back the two bowls, juggling them carefully because of their different sizes. "This is quite an art," she said cheerfully, placing the small bowl in front of me. Steam rose from it, and my stomach lurched. She went back for the bread platter and used a giant fork to lift a chunk onto my rose-patterned plate. Bending over me, she carefully sliced it into ordinary-sized pieces. The jasmine smell mixed with the odor of liquid beef. I swallowed hard.

"I make my own bread," she said. "I can immodestly tell you that I am an excellent cook. You can expect to share some wonderful meals with me. All fresh, healthy ingredients. None of that imitation stuff."

Her big fingers moved awkwardly, but she was efficient. She cut up the bread the way my aunt Myra cuts up food for my three-year-old cousin, Todd. We'd had dinner, she and Uncle Gerry and Todd and Mom and me last Sunday. Tears burned my throat. Just last Sunday. My mom would be freaked. I hadn't come home. Where was I? She'd have called all my friends. The gallery. The police. By now they would have found my bike and my backpack. Unless Mrs. Shepherd had stolen them, too. There'd be a story in the *Times*. Maybe not on the front page, like when McNamara Chang disappeared. He was famous; I wasn't. They might report, "Single parent. Only child. Difficult divorce when Kyle was only two." They'd make it as heartbreaking as possible; that's what newspapers do. Mom's heart would be breaking, no question. I couldn't bear to think about her. Thinking about her made it worse.

"There!" Mrs. Shepherd said when she'd finished. "I hope you won't need salt or pepper. I used to have them on the table, but unfortunately one of your companions once tried to toss some of the pepper into my face. She didn't manage to do it, though. Since then I've decided to be bland rather than blind." She smiled at her joke.

I pushed back my chair, lunged up, and made a dash for the side of her table, knocking over my water glass, slipping on the spill, the leash biting hard into my ankle and jerking me to a stop. My head hung over the edge of the table. It was so high I could have been standing on the roof of a two-story house. I saw one of her feet in her red high-heeled shoes. She'd kicked off the other, and it lay abandoned on its side. My table didn't even move. It was heavy wood, and it had jerked me to a stop, standing there as if rooted, strong as an oak tree.

"GET UP!" She shook with fury. Then she took a breath and smiled indulgently, her voice suddenly sweet. "My dear boy," she said as she reached a hand across to help me stand. "You aren't going to get away. Make up your mind to that, Kyle. Believe me, you'll be more contented if you do. Now why don't you just sit down again and enjoy your nice soup?"

CHAPTER 5

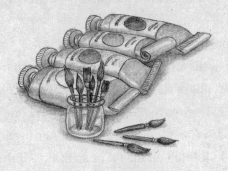

Mrs. Shepherd talked, and

I tried to listen.

She brought custard to the table for dessert when I pushed away the bowl of soup. "This is very light," she said. "Just eggs and milk. Try to eat some of it, Kyle. You'll feel better."

She took a bite of her own. "I'm sure you're wondering exactly what I want with you and the others. Well . . ."

I couldn't help staring at her big tongue that came out to lick a drop of custard off her lips. "When my husband, Magnus, died, I was unbelievably lonely. He was such an intelligent man, such wonderful company, so loving. My best friend. My only friend. We were everything to each other. Perhaps you've heard of him? Dr. Magnus Kroener Shepherd?"

I shook my head.

"Oh, well. Most young people aren't that interested in reading the scientific pages, or the obituaries either. They gave Magnus such a fine one in the *Los Angeles Times*." A tear hung on her eyelid. I sat well back. If it fell on me I'd be soaked. "All the honors," she went on, wiping the tear with her napkin. "But what good are honors to me? He should have won the Nobel Prize. All the scientific community said so. But then . . . committees." She sat twisting her napkin, staring at it. "Such talent. There was nothing he couldn't do. His recent genetic discovery, a miracle really, would have set the world on its ear." She sighed. "Still, now I have you. And McNamara and Tanya, though I'm afraid Tanya was something of a mistake. And then sweet little Lulu. And of course Pippy."

Her voice was determinedly cheerful. "You aren't going to eat? Perhaps you'll take it with you and you can have it later."

I looked at the custard. It had brown speckles on top. Cinnamon probably. My mom made old-fashioned rice pudding dusted with cinnamon that looked like that. I felt like bawling. John Coltrane's music filled the room.

"Is that my mom's CD?"

"I want my Lambkins to be happy. So I brought your music with you." She smiled at me. "Of course I brought your backpack. Your CD player was in it."

"Did you take my bike, too?"

"Oh, yes. I try not to leave anything behind. One must be careful, you know."

She went on, spooning up her custard. "McNamara now, he likes hip-hop, and I have to suffer through that when we have dinner together." She frowned. "Tanya, of course, admits to no preference. But I know what's in her soul. Sometimes I think she believes I play the violin music to taunt her. I would never, never do that."

She pushed back her chair. "So? Would you like to look around before I bring you back?"

I didn't answer. How could she expect me to carry on a conversation when nothing, *nothing* seemed real? I'd never talked to a giant before. She leaned across and unhooked the leash from the table leg, but held it loosely, still attached to my ankle. "I'm sorry to have to keep this on. The thing is, I had too much trust. And in the end that's how John had his accident. I wasn't careful enough, and God knows I blame myself. He—" She stopped. "I think I'll leave the story of John for another day."

She set me down on the floor next to her feet in the red high-heeled shoes. "This is the dining room, of course. My Magnus made all the furniture himself. Woodworking was his hobby. He constructed your house, all of it, inside and out." She stopped to arrange something on a side table. I craned my head back. It was a shell, the biggest shell I ever saw in my life. "The week before he died, we found this on the beach at Dana Point. You'll think this foolish, but sometimes when I hold it to my ear I think I hear Magnus talking to me."

"What does he say?" I croaked.

"He tells me to be strong. To live my life and make the most of it. And that's what I'm doing." She lifted the shell down. "Here. You can listen to the Pacific Ocean." I took some steps backward and she laughed. I could have climbed inside that shell and never been seen again. How could they have found a shell this size? My brain swirled.

"You don't want to listen?" she asked.

I wanted to say something strong and brave. But I wasn't strong, I wasn't brave, and I just shook my head.

"Very well. So let's continue." She set the shell back on the table, caressing it with her hand.

"You may have noticed that Magnus made your house the exact replica of ours," she went on.

"Don't say it's my house." That was better. Not so whiny. "I live in Chatsworth, on Elm Street," I told her, "in an apartment with my mother. She's . . ." Strong and brave, yeah right. In a minute I'd be blubbering. I stretched the leash as far as it would go, but that wasn't far. *Tight rein*, I thought. I'd never known, really, what that meant. Now I did. I twisted and strained against it, and she murmured, "Easy, Kyle. Easy, honey," the way you'd say it to a frantic dog or a horse. I struggled and struggled while she held on and watched. Sweat beaded my forehead. I stood, legs apart, panting.

"You know what, Kyle," she said gently. "I think you've had just about enough for one day. I was going to show you the rest of the house, to share with you all the wonders of my Magnus. But I think

I'll just take you to the children's room. You'll find it interesting."

She led, almost dragged, me along a corridor. I skidded on the wooden floor, not even trying to walk. I had a dog once, Nellie, who used to sit down when we were out and she got tired or stubborn. I would have sat down now, except that I didn't want to be picked up again and carried. Nellie had always liked that, but I didn't want it.

The dust on the baseboards made me sneeze. It looked to be about a half-inch deep, thick and whiskery. Our passing turned it into a miniature dust storm.

"God bless you," Mrs. Shepherd said.

She stopped at a white painted door. When I looked way up, I saw that it was covered with decals of moons and stars and rainbows. It had a glittering glass doorknob. The children's room?

She opened the door.

"Look," she said. "These were my darlings before I got you!"

In the room were four giant-sized dolls. One girl was dressed in party clothes. One wore tennis whites and carried a racket. She was smiling a painted smile. A male doll wore leather pants and boots. The other had on shorts and a striped T-shirt.

Mrs. Shepherd beamed down at me. "What do you think, Kyle?" She pointed. "This is Betsy, this is Britney. The dark guy is Victor, and the one in shorts is Brian. Aren't they wonderful?"

I couldn't have spoken if I'd tried. I was numb. These dolls were huge, as big as I was.

"Did—did Magnus make these for you?" I whispered at last.

Nothing seemed impossible anymore.

"Heavens, no." She bent down and righted Betsy, who had tipped over. "But he made the house for them. You know, your house. And then, after he passed and I was alone, they weren't quite enough for me. I needed living dolls, not just lifelike ones. Real children."

"Living dolls?" My voice seemed to be coming out of a tin can.

"So I removed them from their home and turned it over to you." She sounded smug, as if this had been a smart move on her part.

I felt myself sway.

Mrs. Shepherd looked down. "Oh, my poor little Lambkin. All this is too much for you to assimilate. I'm going to take you home now."

She picked me up.

"Forgive me for tiring you out. I was just so happy to have you join me . . . us."

She closed the moon-and-stars door carefully behind us and stalked back along the corridor, talking, always talking.

"I must tell you, Kyle, that you have nothing to fear. I will never hurt you or any of my little Lambkins. I love you. The four of you are what I live for now. You can be happy here, as long as you behave. And Kyle . . ." She stopped talking and held me high, so that our faces almost touched. Her lips were rimmed with scarlet, but the insides were white as slugs where her lipstick had washed off. "And Kyle, there's a lovely surprise waiting for you when you go back." She squeezed my waist, which I thought was probably supposed to be affection. She almost cracked my ribs. "You are going to be so excited."

"I don't think so," I muttered.

My dish of custard was still on the table, skinned over now, disgusting.

"Do you want to take it?" she asked, and I shook my head.

She picked up my shoes from the floor, gave

them to me, and set me on the edge of her table so I could put them on. My fingers didn't seem to belong to me.

She slid her hand into her glove and picked me up.

"Here we go," she said softly as she carried me home.

CHAPTER 6

She carried me down the steps. It was dark now, but she switched on a low-watt yellow light that let us see our way into what I supposed was a basement. This time I was upright in her fist, but it was still sickening. Every jolt as she stepped down was like being on an airplane that had hit an air pocket. My insides bounced.

I saw the house from above as we came toward it. It was an ordinary flat-roofed bungalow, the white paint washed a sickly yellow in the light from the bulb. No chimney. No lawn in front. No trees. Above the house was a street lamp on a long pole that arched across the roof. There was no sign of life inside. But how could there be? There were no windows, no doors.

Mrs. Shepherd reached up to the top of the street lamp, clicked a button. A bright light came on.

"That's better," she said.

I tried to lift my hand to shade my eyes, but both hands were trapped inside her fist. The glare of white light could have been from a halogen lamp.

There were no shadows.

She rapped on the flat roof with her knuckles, then, one-handed, undid the clips and lifted off the roof.

I could see inside now, a seagull view from above. The house was lit as if with a searchlight, every corner illuminated.

"Good evening, my Lambkins," she called cheerfully. For a few seconds I saw the three of them and Pippy. Tanya was on the couch with her arm around Lulu, their faces turned up to watch. Pippy lay curled beside them. She lifted her head and barked ferociously, twice, then wagged her tail and settled down again into sleep. Mac was in another room, bent over a desk or a table.

There was a quick *whish* of air around me as

Mrs. Shepherd set me down on the rug. My bird's-eye view had disappeared.

I stood, groggy, disoriented, rubbing my eyes.

Her voice came again from above us. "Tanya? Do you have everything you need for the night?"

Tanya didn't lift her head. She made a sound that could have meant yes.

"Lulu, pet. Did you have a nice dinner? Did Tanya give you some of the nice soup and salad I fixed for you?"

Lulu looked up and nodded. "The soup was good. And we had custard."

"Excellent, darling. Did you drink a glass of milk?"

"Yes. And Mac made a face on the custard for me with some of yesterday's cherries and it was funny."

"That's good, precious. McNamara is so nice."

I made myself look up and saw the huge face, filling the space again, the bright light behind her making her too-red hair even redder.

"McNamara?" she called. "Did you get a lot done today?"

"Quite a bit," he called back. "It's going well."

I heard the smile in her voice. "That's what I like to hear. Well then, I think I'll say good night. See you in the morning."

There was a dull thud as the roof was laid back on. I counted ten clicks as the clips were snapped into place. Her high-heeled red shoes *tap-tapped* on the steps. Then silence.

"Would you like a glass of water?" Tanya asked me.

I nodded and dropped down into one of the big chairs. My sides and ribs throbbed. Small hammers thumped inside my head.

Lulu came and stood in front of me. She was sucking her thumb again. Mac came, too, from wherever he'd been. For the first time I noticed that his eyes were a bright, clear blue, odd looking in his Asian face.

"Are you all right?" he asked.

"I guess so," I said. "I don't know what happened. I don't know what's real and what isn't."

Tanya was back with the water. "It's all real. Believe it."

They watched me as I drank. The water was lukewarm, stale tasting, but I was glad for it.

"Would someone explain it to me then?" I asked.

Mac sat down on the rug, and Lulu came to sit beside him. "How much did she tell you?" he asked.

"I don't know. Mostly all about Magnus. And how he built this house."

"Magnus the Magnificent," Tanya said spitefully. "It's all his fault."

"Well, to be fair, he didn't know she'd do something like this," Mac said.

Tanya shrugged.

I took a deep breath. "I'm still not getting it. You mean, because he was a scientist he taught her how to turn herself into a giant?"

Tanya looked at Mac, then said: "You've got the wrong end of the stick, Kyle. He didn't turn her into a giantess. She shrunk us."

"What are you talking about?" I sat straight in the chair, staring from one of them to the other.

"She shrunked us," Lulu said. "We're little, little, little. Littler than anything, almost."

"She doesn't like the word 'shrunk,'" Mac said. "She thinks it's vulgar."

"And Mrs. Shepherd can't stand anything vulgar," Tanya added.

"She much prefers 'reduced.' Or even 'diminished.' Like in 'before I diminished you.'" Tanya's voice was a booming parody of Mrs. Shepherd's.

"No way. We're just the same. Look, how—"

"We're not just the same," Mac said quietly. "We can think we are when we're in here, together. But outside of here, in her house, we're miniscule. And if we were in the real world . . ." He spread his hands.

"I thought she had a giant house that fit her. And that we were . . ." I looked for words and had trouble finding them. "I thought we were ordinary normal human size."

"Not anymore."

"She took us and she made us the size she could handle. She's keeping us," Tanya said.

"But why? This is crazy. It can't be true."

"It's because she loves us," Lulu said. "I told you. She does everything to make us happy. Except if we're bad. She gets scary." She put her thumb in her mouth, took it out again, and said, "Except I'm hardly ever bad, right, Tanya?"

Tanya nodded. "Right."

"Mrs. Shepherd's teaching me to be Shirley Temple," Lulu added. "Do you know who Shirley Temple is, Kyle?"

I nodded. What had Shirley Temple got to do with all this?

"The Shepherd's wacko, that's all," Tanya said.

I stood up. My legs were still wobbly, and I held on to the back of the velvet chair. My mind buzzed. This couldn't be true. I lifted my hand and examined it. It was the same, the right size for a hand, exactly the way it had always been. But I was remembering things from today. Things that had seemed puzzling at the time. The shell that they'd found on the beach at Dana Point. You would never find shells that size on the beach at Dana Point. But what if it was a regular shell and I was the little creature looking at it? Shivers ran along my skin. The little creature who could have climbed inside it.

And then there were the giant dolls.

"She showed me the dolls," I said at last. "I wondered how she got such big ones."

"Oh, yes, the dolls. She collected them before she learned how to collect us." Tanya rolled her eyes. "Totally wacko, like I told you. At least we get to wear their clothes, and believe me, those dolls have some good-looking outfits."

"But we'll grow back to being ourselves, won't we?" I was pleading now, pleading for them to say, "Yes. Sure we will."

"We won't, if she can help it," Tanya said. "Every week we get a shot. She tells us they're vitamin shots, but we've figured it out. They keep us this size. Come in the kitchen and we'll show you how we found out."

I followed her down the corridor and through a door into a dining room exactly the same as Mrs. Shepherd's had been.

"It's just the same—" I began.

Tanya looked over her shoulder. "I know." She clicked on a lamp.

Mac and Lulu trailed us as we went through the dining room into a kitchen. Pippy bounded off the couch and trotted after us, tail wagging.

"No, Pippy. It's not dinnertime. You've had your food," Lulu scolded, and she scooped her up and carried her. I stared at the dog. Had she been "diminished," too?

The kitchen had open cupboards filled with plastic dishes. Mac saw me looking at them. "Doll tea sets," he said. "I guess they make all kinds of stuff for dollhouses nowadays."

"Always did," Tanya said. "I remember."

"You're saying we're living in a dollhouse?" My voice was rising, like a maniac's, and I coughed to cover it.

"Sure. A bigger-than-usual one. He made it for her dolls," Tanya said. "And we're their size. We have four bedrooms. 'Four bedrooms for four dolls. Children should have their privacy.'" Now she was mimicking Mrs. Shepherd's voice again. It was uncanny how much she sounded like her.

I saw a stove, a refrigerator, a sink, and I pointed. "Dolls' appliances?"

Tanya nodded. "They don't work. They did once. Magnus the Magnificent was smart enough for that. Awhile back we had electricity all over. No more."

I glanced at the lamp Mac had just turned on.

"Batteries." He answered my question before I spoke it. "Some people made sure that we won't be trusted."

I noticed a black, burned portion of the wall behind the stove and pointed to it.

"Yep," Tanya said. "John and I took a piece of Mac's paper and tried to set a fire, but she saw the smoke. Or maybe smelled it."

"She was soooo angry!" Lulu whispered. "She shook all over. Like this." Lulu jiggled, and Pippy jiggled with her.

"Next day our electricity was shut off," Tanya said. "She hated to do it, of course. She wants us to be comfortable. But if we misbehave, there are consequences." She slumped against the wall. "Except sometimes there are no consequences. It keeps us guessing. She likes that."

"At least she didn't confiscate my paper," Mac added.

Tanya rolled her eyes. "Big deal."

"It is to me," Mac snapped.

"When we had the fire," Lulu went on, "there was all this big smoke." She set Pippy down so she could make wide, billowing motions with her arms. "Mrs. Shepherd looked through the roof and she had this big red extinguisher and she squeezed it and it went *poof*!" Lulu puffed out her cheeks. "And it blew out the fire. Mrs. Shepherd said it was so dangerous. If we'd had a fire it would have burned us all up and there is no way to get out."

"What good would it have been if we'd burned ourselves to death?" Mac muttered under his breath.

"We wanted her to get so flustered that she'd grab us all at one time. Something she never does, by the way. And maybe we could have scattered and gotten free," Tanya said.

"Kind of a big risk, though," I muttered.

Tanya raised her eyebrows. "When you're here awhile, big risks are worth taking. You'll see."

I noticed how Mac had stayed out of this conversation. It was obvious he and Tanya didn't agree. He didn't seem to think the risks were worth taking.

"The fire was John's plan," Tanya said. "John was great. He was ready to try anything."

"And look where it got him," Mac said.

"Be quiet, Mac," Tanya said sharply.

Mac shook his head. "I'm only telling the truth," he muttered.

What's with him? I wondered. He was older. He should have been the leader here.

"Well, I have to get out," I said. "There's no way I'm going to stay, living in a dollhouse. Mac, can't you do something . . ." My voice was cracking and I stopped.

They were all quiet. Mac looked away.

Lulu picked up Pippy and cradled her. "John was awful sick. We had a funeral for him when he died. It was nice. Mrs. Shepherd played his music."

Tanya leaned against the kitchen counter and refilled my cup. Water trickled out of the faucet.

"Magnus the Magnificent," Tanya said. "Only cold water, though. Forget about warm showers."

"There are showers, too?"

"Freezing ones," Mac said.

Tanya walked to the door. There were marks on the wood.

"Here's what I want to show you. These are our

heights. Here's mine. I'm usually five foot two. This was John's. He said that once he was five-eleven. This is Mac's, six foot one. This is Lulu's, three foot one."

"And way down there is Pippy's," Lulu interrupted.

Tanya smiled. "Now, look, see these marks a little above the others? About a quarter-inch higher?"

I nodded.

"We grew that much when she was two days late with the injections. That was when she went to take you."

That day! I remembered it clearly now. School. Algebra. We got back our tests. Recess. Eating with Jason. Going to the gallery, stopping to check the window like I always did. I wanted to see my painting again. It blew me away every time I saw it there, knowing people looked in this window, talked about the paintings. But mine had vanished. Oh, no! What had happened? They couldn't have taken away my prize, could they? Going inside then, and Richard coming over to me. Finding out about the sale.

I was shivering all over. How could this have happened so fast?

Tanya was still telling about our heights, about shots. I had to concentrate. "Somehow taking you didn't happen as quickly as Mrs. S thought it would, and she wasn't back in time. So instead of a Saturday, she gave the shots to us on the next Tuesday, yesterday."

"You mean—you mean, if we don't get those shots we start to grow again?"

"And it's fast," Tanya added. "That much in two days!" She measured with her finger and thumb a little apart. "I figure at that rate, without the shots we could be back to normal-person size in five or six months."

"So," I began, "if we can stop her from giving them—"

"Exactly," Tanya said. "The thing is to find a way."

"There must be one." I was feeling better. There was a possibility.

"Don't be getting his hopes up, Tanya," Mac said.

Tanya gave him a cold stare. "Meantime, Kyle," she said, "want to stand over here? Let's get your size."

I stood with my back to the wood while she took a plastic knife from the knife drawer and made a mark with the others.

My height was between John's and Tanya's.

"How tall are we now?" My voice shook.

"Picture a bottle of Coke, more or less," Tanya said. "And I don't mean supersize."

I looked at the mark that was me and I got this terrible, panicky feeling.

Now I was a registered Coke bottle–sized Lambkin.

CHAPTER 7

Tanya and Lulu showed

me the rest of the dollhouse. Mac had taken off, muttering something about getting back to work.

"Go for it!" Tanya said flatly. "Think of all the time you've already wasted this morning."

"What work does he do?" I couldn't imagine. What was there to do if we couldn't go outside? Housework maybe? A hobby?

"Mac's writing a book," Lulu said. "Not storybooks like Mrs. Shepherd reads to me. He's writing a big, big book." She nodded vigorously, and her black curls bounced. "Mac really likes to write."

"He's obsessed, you mean." Tanya gave a little

shiver. "Nothing else matters but his novel." She said the word "novel" in capital letters, then added, "Sorry! I shouldn't be so mean. It's just . . ." She didn't finish the sentence.

I thought for a minute. "Maybe he's lucky. Maybe it gets him through this."

Tanya gave me a sharp look. "It doesn't help the rest of us much," she said.

"But he's older. He's been here longer. I'd think he'd have worked something out."

"He hasn't," Tanya said. "You don't know how he is." Then, "Come on, let's show you the house. Magnus the Magnificent did a good job, I have to say. At least we don't have to live in some crummy dump. We'll skip Mac's room. He doesn't like to be disturbed. It's so insane! As if his life isn't make-believe enough."

I followed them along a corridor, and she opened a door. There were plenty of inside doors, I noticed. It was just ones leading to the outside that were missing.

"This is my room," Lulu said proudly. "These are all my stuffed animals, Monkey and Crocodile, and Bunny and . . ." She lifted them, one after another. Most were just the right size for her. I imagined Mrs. Shepherd combing the toy stores, picking out the most miniature stuffed animals she could find.

"For my little granddaughter," she might say to the smiling clerk. Goose bumps rose along my arms and legs.

A giant teddy bear in a tattered red vest and raggedy black trousers lay on Lulu's bed, almost covering it. Pippy jumped up beside him, circled him, sniffed loudly, then jumped back down.

"This is Old Bear," Lulu said.

"She dropped him when the Shepherd took her. The Shepherd threw him in her car," Tanya explained. "But she couldn't get him to shrink. She can only bring down something that's attached to us. Like our clothes."

"Mrs. Shepherd said it was okay if I kept him. He's my old friend." Lulu trailed him off the bed, her little arms not even able to circle his waist.

"Here, sweetheart, I'll help." Tanya reached around him from the other side. Lulu stood for a minute, hugging him with Tanya's help. He was bigger in every way than she was.

"I've had him since I was a tiny baby," Lulu told me. "Mrs. Shepherd kept him for me because she wants me to be happy."

I nodded. "I'm glad you got to keep him anyway, Lulu." If only I'd had my cell phone in my pants pocket! But it was in my backpack along with my CDs. Which meant Mrs. Shepherd had it, too, along with my CDs. She had it! Maybe I could get to it somehow. Mac didn't want me to get my hopes up, but I had to have some kind of hope or I'd go nuts.

We were in Tanya's room now. It was modern, all cheerful bedcovers and bright oversized pillows that littered the floor. They were probably ordinary size, small even. I was having trouble keeping things straight, translating from large to small and back again. Would it have been better if Mrs. Shepherd had really been a giant and we'd been normal size? Much better. What chance did we have as mini-midgets?

"I forgot," I said. "She told me there was a lovely surprise waiting for me."

"I guess you like to paint," Tanya said. She opened a door. "Here's your lovely surprise."

The room where I was to sleep had a single-size bed. *Doll bed*, I thought, and I closed my eyes tight and shook my head. I had to pretend, try to believe, that this was a normal house and normal kids were living in it. Had this been John's room before he had his accident and his funeral? Four kids, four rooms; one kid goes, another one comes. That was the way Mrs. Shepherd worked it. I vaguely noticed the red chenille bedcover and that one of the walls was painted an almost-red, too. But what really grabbed my attention were the canvases that leaned against the red wall, canvases of all sizes and all shapes. I could tell just by looking at them that they were already primed. On a table next to them were tubes of oil paint, so large they covered the top. From the entrance to the room, I could read the print on them. There was a jar of brushes. Where did she get brushes this size? She must have made them herself so they would be just right for me, the size I was now. There was a plastic palette, wooden sticks for mixing, and small jars of colorless liquid that could be linseed oil. The room was better equipped than the corner of the bedroom I had at home. As good, almost, as the gallery.

I walked across to the brushes and I couldn't

help it. I picked one up, weighed it in my hand, felt the smooth varnished texture of the handle, ran my fingers across the ends of the bristles. My heart started to thump, the way it always does when I'm ready to paint.

"Here we go," Tanya said.

I turned to look at her. She had the prettiest almond-shaped eyes, but right now they were hard as pebbles. "You're probably going to be lost in painting the way Mac is in his writing. You won't be interested in anything else, not even getting out of here. Not even wanting to help. The Shepherd knows how to keep her Lambkins happy."

I put the brush back in the jar. "That won't ever happen."

I'd paint again. But not here. I'd get out of this nightmare first, somehow.

Lulu's lips quivered. "Mrs. Shepherd's nice to me. But I want my mama. And I want my papa. My papa is the best papa in the whole world. I just want to go home."

"I don't have a home. Not one that I care about," Tanya said. "But I swear, I will never complain again if I can just get out of here."

"There has to be a way." I sat on the edge of the bed that was to be mine. On the wall beside it was a faded patch in the paint where, I guessed, a poster had hung. The patch was the right size and shape. Of course a real poster would cover this entire wall. I gave my head a small shake. I'd never get used to thinking this way.

"John had a postcard up there," Tanya said. "Courtesy of Mrs. Shepherd. She took it down . . . after."

"It was a picture of a man called Caruso," Lulu said. "He was a famous singer. Like John."

"Oh." John had been a singer. "What kind of singer?" I asked.

"Opera mostly," Tanya said. "He could sing just about anything, but he liked opera best. That's what he wanted to do, and he was on his way when she . . . when she took him. He'd auditioned at the Oberlin Conservatory of Music in Ohio. They were all set to give him a partial scholarship. But that wasn't going to work out because his parents couldn't come up with the rest of the money. I know John would have made it some way. I'm a hundred percent sure. Naturally, the Shepherd thought he'd be better with her. She said she might even get him a voice coach." Tanya snorted. "John said he'd never open his mouth if that happened. Imagine, she'd have had to shrink some poor voice coach and overcrowd her precious house."

"Sometimes John sang the clown song for us," Lulu said solemnly. "But the clown was sad. Sometimes John cried."

The red bedcover smelled as if it had been washed in something soft and sweet. My mom has a blue robe made of this kind of stuff. She wears it in the mornings when she's fixing breakfast, before we both leave. Nausea rose in my throat. "There has to be a way," I repeated.

Tanya picked up Pippy. "You think we haven't tried everything?"

"You said about the needle that she uses for the shots. We'll figure out how to get it and—"

"Oh, yeah? How? To us that needle is big as a baton. And we're leashed. Always leashed since John made his move. And you can believe she keeps that butterfly net right at hand."

"Maybe we can get the net. Put it over her head. Trap her."

"Tried it," Tanya said. "Even John couldn't lift that net. And there are never two of us up there with her when she's needle-sticking us. Or anytime, for that matter."

"Tanya bit Mrs. Shepherd once," Lulu said. "On her big thumb. Mrs. Shepherd squealed."

Tanya grinned. "My one sweet memory. She squealed and dropped me. On the roof, just before she lifted it off. I'm running like a hound, round and round that roof, and that giant hand of hers is chasing after me, making great grabs, and I'm, like, dancing away. But she caught me, of course. There was nowhere to go. She was dripping great drops of blood. A gorgeous sight. But she cornered me and picked me up. From then on, she's worn a glove. It's like we're hawks and she doesn't want our claws in her. If I had claws, they'd be tearing at her, believe me."

"Mrs. Shepherd said Tanya's bite hurt real bad," Lulu said.

Tanya nodded. "She actually asked what she'd done that made me so vicious. The weirdo thinks we should be grateful to her."

"Did she . . . do something to you, Tanya?" I asked. "I mean, punish you or—"

Lulu's eyes widened. "She did. First she growled and growled. We could hear her. Oh, I hate it when she does that. Then . . ." She stopped. "Then she bitted Tanya!"

"She *bit* you!" My voice shook.

"She sure did." Tanya nudged up the sleeve of her T-shirt. "Right here."

I saw the scar of the tooth marks, like five angry spots close to her shoulder.

"She just grabbed me up and—" Tanya gnashed her teeth. "Like this. Lucky for me she didn't actually clamp down. I'd have been armless. She said, 'You do it to me, I'll do it to you.' It hurt like blazes. I was afraid the venom in her might have poisoned me, but as you see, I got over it."

"Mrs. Shepherd gave Tanya cream and a bandage to put on it," Lulu said. "She was kind after, wasn't she, Tanya?"

"Real kind," Tanya said. "It's like, you know, the cobra strikes, then smiles."

I couldn't help letting my eyes shift past her to the paint and the brushes and those canvases. I made myself look away from them and saw that Tanya was staring at me, so I stood up quickly and began examining the walls all the way around the room, touching each corner, getting down on my knees on the wooden floor, lifting up the edges of the red bedspread.

Tanya watched, her shoulders slumped. "What are you looking for? A trapdoor? A secret opening with a corridor behind it that leads to I-5?"

"What about digging a tunnel?" I asked.

"We only have plastic knives around here. No glass, either, in case we would break it and make good use of the broken pieces."

I stared at the ceiling, thinking out loud. "She comes up and down those stone steps. What about a trip wire at the top?"

Tanya took a deep breath. "Don't I wish. I'd love to see her fall from top to bottom, but there's no way to do it. There's nothing you can think of that we haven't thought of already. And tried. At least John and I have." She snuggled her face into Pippy's neck.

"Are you saying there's no use trying anymore? We just have to live here, like—like zombies?"

"Mac says we should try to accept." Lulu pronounced it "ezpect." "He says we should try to be as calm as we can because we make it worse for ourselves, being sad all the time. He says an opportunity will come."

"He's okay with being here," Tanya said.

"What do you mean?" My voice was rising. "How can he be okay?"

"He's got his writing. He has plenty of time now, something he never had before. He's lost in it, hour after hour, day after day. Then he gets to read it to her, chapter by chapter, when she takes him up for dinner. She's interested. He won't read to us."

"Do you know what it's about?"

"He sort of told John and me once. It's about ancient Ireland. About the kings and the warriors and the druids and giants. Stuff like that. And us with our very own giant!"

"There are fairies, too," Lulu added. "But some of them are bad fairies."

"He's part Irish," Tanya said, and I remembered the blue eyes.

We were silent.

"What happened to John?" I asked at last.

Tanya looked quickly at Lulu and then back at

me, and I understood I wasn't to ask the details. Not right now.

"Can you get us out, Kyle?" Lulu whispered. "I really, really, really want to go home."

She should have been asking Mac. I bet she had already. But that hadn't worked. Now she was depending on me. How scary was that?

"I'll get you out." I put my hand over hers and squeezed gently. "I promise."

CHAPTER 8

Later that night, Tanya and Mac and I tucked Lulu into bed, Pippy on one side of her, Old Bear on the other. We each had to lean over and kiss all three of them good night. Old Bear stared up at us, his glass eyes as big as Ping-Pong balls, his paws neatly arranged outside the blankets.

"Will you sing to me, Tanya?" Lulu asked sleepily. "The song about love."

"Not tonight, sweetheart." Tanya brushed the dark curls off Lulu's forehead. "You know I'm not much of a singer. Not like John."

"I like it when you sing to me," Lulu whispered. She smiled up at me. "I'm glad you've come, Kyle."

I swallowed. "Thank you, Lulu."

We tiptoed away.

"She doesn't really understand," Tanya said to me. "She doesn't get it that she shouldn't be glad you're here. Because now you're in the same awful mess as the rest of us."

"She doesn't get the concept of forever," Mac added.

I stared at him. "I don't get it either. Do you?"

We went back in the living room. "Would anyone like a glass of juice?" Tanya asked. "It's warm," she told me. "The Shepherd brings it to us cold every morning, but by now it's not too great."

"You get used to it," Mac said.

I shrugged. No point in saying what I'd just about said before. I wasn't going to be here long enough to get used to anything. There had to be a way out, and I'd find it.

"I'll pass on the juice," I said.

Then, "You don't read Lulu a bedtime story?" I asked, just to break the silence.

Tanya flopped onto the couch. "What would we read? I have some of those little books. The Shepherd gave them to me, so I'd be calmer or sweeter tempered. You know the kind. *Wise*

Sayings of Confucius. A Woman's Guide to Peace of Mind. Lulu's not too interested when I try reading them to her. I'm not too interested myself. Sometimes I tell her a story that I remember. Or sometimes she tells us one that the Shepherd has read to her."

"*Frog and Toad* or *The Runaway Bunny*," Mac added. "She's told us that one a gazillion times."

I sat down on the couch next to Tanya, but Mac still stood. Tanya smelled of soap. Her skin was the color of coffee without cream, rich and strong.

"Well." Mac shuffled his feet. I sensed the impatience in him, the itch to get away. All of him seemed to lean toward his bedroom.

"I hear you're writing a novel," I said.

He smiled a great, happy smile.

"It's actually a trilogy," he said. "I'm on book two."

His face was suddenly flushed with pleasure. How could he be contented? Was he able to accept that word "forever" so easily?

"What's it about? Your trilogy?"

"It's a historical, true fantasy."

"There's such a thing?"

"Probably not. But who's to tell me that, in here?"

"I've never been much into fantasy," I told him. "*Lord of the Rings*. The hobbits and Frodo, stuff like that. I never did finish those books."

I heard myself talking about *Lord of the Rings*, and it was totally unreal. Not just *Lord of the Rings*, but the fact that I was having such an ordinary conversation.

"A lot of people don't care for it," Mac said. "But a lot of people do."

There was that smile again, not patronizing, just understanding. I was looking up at him, actually seeing him clearly for the first time. He was long and lanky, not shaped like a baseball player at all. I vaguely remembered local sports commentators saying: "Whoever heard of a six-foot-one pitcher? But hey, folks, the mixture works." It had definitely worked. I studied him some more. His face was broad and flat with high cheekbones and wide, curving lips. He had a wispy little beard, and I decided he definitely looked Chinese, but then there were those blue eyes. And that name, McNamara.

"I thought you were only interested in baseball," I said.

His smile vanished. "Not by choice."

"Oh."

The conversation had died. "Well, I guess I'll get back to book two," Mac said.

"Do that," Tanya told him.

We sat in an uncomfortable quiet when he'd gone.

"Are you always mad at him like this?" I asked. "Is it just because he's so into his writing?"

"I think he kisses up to her when he writes and when he reads to her at dinner," Tanya said. "She loves it. I think she praises his book to the skies and he comes back all pleased with himself. John couldn't handle him doing that." She paused. "I guess you're an artist. She'll be praising your pictures, encouraging you. She has this stupid idea that she's a patron of the arts."

"Actually, I'm not an artist," I said. "Only sort of. I mean, I want to be." For a second I almost told her about selling one of my paintings, but I didn't.

"She knows you want to be. She's tempting you with those paints. If you really want to destroy her, you won't even screw the tops off the tubes. She was furious with me when I wouldn't do the stuff she'd planned for me to do."

69

"You mean like play chess with her?"

"That. And 'engaging in good conversation.'"
Tanya made a face. "Blah, blah, blah. I just sit and
stare at her. She's all the time telling me how much
I've disappointed her. Now she can be furious with
you, too. She can't let either of us go, of course. So
she's stuck with us. And then there was John." I
noticed the soft, sweet sadness in her voice when she
spoke John's name.

"Can you tell me about him now?" I asked hesi-
tantly.

"He was . . ." I heard her take a raggedy breath.
"John was wonderful, in every way. Brave and fear-
less and smart. He was older than me. John was . . .
he was a big brother to us, me and Lulu. He tried to
keep our spirits up. He protected us as best he could.
He never lost faith." She paused. "And he could sing
like an angel."

I thought for a minute that Tanya wouldn't be
able to go on. "He wouldn't sing for her, no matter
how much she pleaded or bribed. He just wouldn't.
He was like a rock. I didn't want him to do what
he did in the end. I begged him not to try. He said he
didn't care how dangerous it was, he had to make
another effort."

I turned toward her on the couch as we talked, but she never looked at me. She was making circles with her fingers on the knees of her blue jeans. Betsy jeans, Britney jeans, size zero, zero, zero. She glanced up at me once, as if feeling my eyes on her, then looked back at her fingers, concentrating on those circles. I concentrated on them, too.

"I asked John, 'What about me? How will I go on here without you, with only little Lulu and Pippy and Mac who doesn't care about anything but his writing? Who's going to look after us?'"

I wanted to say something, but I couldn't think of anything. Except "Well, I'm here now," and that would be no comfort. I waited through the silence.

" 'I'll come back and save all of you, I promise,' John said. He came back in a nice wooden box, the kind you use to store CDs. She'd painted his name on the side, John Ponderelli, and the date he died."

"How *did* he die?"

"It was his turn to go up to have dinner with her. He hated that. He wouldn't eat. He wouldn't talk. She played him all the music he loved, Pavarotti, Leone Magiera arias from his favorite operas. The Shepherd didn't have leashes on us when we ate then. Just when we walked." Tanya looked up, and her eyes were as dull as her voice. "She walks us outside every day so we can get air and exercise. Like dogs. But always one at a time." She paused, and I watched the tightening of her face as she pulled back her thoughts. "John was sitting at the table on her table. You know how she works it?"

I nodded.

"No leash. While she was eating he jumped up, grabbed his chair, which is super heavy, and ran at her, holding it—you know the way lion tamers hold a chair in front of them, with the legs straight out?"

I nodded again.

"He rammed the chair legs right into her face. His plan was to hurt her bad, then to swarm down the big, thick leg of her table, and get away some-how. It didn't happen that way."

I waited.

"He ran at her, holding the chair, and he thrust it right at her eyes, he didn't care if it blinded her . . ." She looked up at me, and I saw her tears.

"She swiped at him and the chair, I guess with

the back of her hand. She swept him off the table, and she's so strong he went flying all the way across to the opposite wall. He crashed into it."

The tears ran unchecked down her cheeks now.

"He broke just about everything inside of him. No doctor, of course. No ambulance taking him to the emergency room. Just the Shepherd wringing her hands and being sorry. *Sorry!*"

I didn't say anything. Whatever I said would have been lame and insulting.

I'd never been in a silence exactly like this one. No music, no voices. No ticking clock or humming refrigerator. No outside sound of traffic or birds or crickets. Just blankness.

"How do you know what happened?" I asked at last.

"She told us. I knew what he was going to try, of course. John was strong. Every day we all do push-ups and sit-ups. He could do a hundred, no sweat. He prepared. Of course, it doesn't matter what we do in the end. She's bigger and stronger and tougher. We're like a bunch of puny gnats to her. Afterward she described it all to us. She sobbed, wailed. She kept saying how devastated she was. Devastated. Her word. She said how much she'd loved John. How much she loved all of us. One of her eyes was red and purple for about a week, and she had Band-Aids on her cheeks. John definitely connected, before—"

Her head drooped.

"She wanted to know what else she could do to make us accept the way things were now, here. I screamed at her. I looked up at her big face filling the roof, and if I'd had a gun I would have shot her dead. 'Just give me a gun, you freak,' I screamed at her. 'That's all you can do for me.'"

Her nose was running now, too. She let it run and mix with her tears, but I had no tissue to give her and no idea where to get one.

"Anyway," she said. "Now we're leashed when we dine. She's upset about that. It spoils the ambience."

She took a deep, shuddery breath, sighed, and looked at her watch. It was a man's silver one with a thick bracelet chain that was too loose on her wrist. Had it been John's? Had he given it to her before he went on his dangerous mission? Or had the Shepherd given it to her, afterward?

"I think I'll go to bed," she said wearily. "You know where your room is."

I stood. "Not my room. My room is at home."

She smiled. All at once I felt brave, as if I could do anything.

I heard her go into the bathroom, then into the room that she slept in. There were some small sounds of a drawer opening and closing. Then I was surrounded again by that awful, numbing silence.

CHAPTER 9

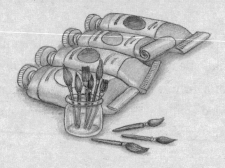

I collapsed back onto the couch. Tanya's words rang in my ears. "It doesn't matter what we do. . . . She's bigger and stronger." There was such a finality to them. Could she be right? That I'd be here, we'd all be here, for the rest of our lives? Lulu wouldn't get bigger. Would we grow old? Would we get fatter, thinner, more miserable, year after year? Or did the drug that kept us small keep us young forever? Suddenly I couldn't breathe.

I jumped up. How had this happened to me? I tried to make my mind function. I'd been coming home from the gallery, along Anney's Road, the way I came every Tuesday and Thursday night. The

Shepherd must have known that. She *had* been stalking me. My skin crawled. But why me? I wasn't important. And then there was this feeling I had that I'd seen her someplace before. That red, red hair, the color of a clown's.

I had to use the bathroom.

The toilet flushed slowly and noisily. Hardly any water. I looked down into it. Everything was a possible escape route now. There must be a pipe. Had the others already tried this? There was just a small hole at the bottom of the bowl, no larger than a golf ball. Only a trickle came out of the faucet of the washbasin when I turned it on. No way down that drain. Even my finger, my tiny, tiny finger, wouldn't fit into it.

Was Mac still writing there in his room, totally lost in the world of early Ireland?

I knocked on his door.

For a few seconds I thought he might be in bed, asleep. But he was at his desk. The way he looked around at me I could tell he was bringing himself back from another place, a place filled with his imagination. But his wide, curving smile was friendly.

"Hi," I said. "Is it okay if I interrupt you?"

"Sure." He ran his hands through his hair.

"I wanted to ask you," I said. "Has anyone tried going down through the toilet? There must be a pipe. . . ."

He grinned. "Tanya tried. She got stuck. I shouldn't laugh, but she was so determined. Of course there was no way. Fortunately she'd gone in feet first and we were able to pull her out. The only thing hurt was her pride, and she's got a heck of a lot of that."

"I guessed! Another thing?" I asked. "When Mrs. Shepherd lifts off the roof, have you tried rushing her, all at one time? I mean, pushing up on the roof, knocking her off balance?"

"Tried. We piled up the furniture and stood on top and shoved the minute the clips were off. She just clamped down and locked the roof back on. She's got the strength of ten. Of us, anyway." He looked at me sympathetically. "There's no way to get the better of this woman." I watched him roll his neck, stretching it, watched him flex his fingers.

"I cramp sometimes," he said.

I took a step toward the desk where papers were piled. They looked like ordinary-size typing paper, but I was getting the hang of this. Either Mrs.

Shepherd had cut them down to manageable size, or she'd bought the kind of loose sheets you leave at a phone, for quick messages.

"She started me off with notebooks," Mac said, watching me. "But we pulled out the staples and she quickly realized they could be a danger. So now I just have separate sheets." He ruffled the edges with his finger. "But I'm thankful."

I nodded.

"You must be a budding artist," he said. It wasn't a question. "That's why she took you."

"I haven't budded much yet," I said quickly.

"She bought you the canvases and paint."

"I won't be using them," I said, and he looked at me closely.

"Don't let Tanya shame you into that. You'll be here for a long time. If you love to paint, do. Otherwise you'll go nuts."

I leaned against the doorjamb. "What did you mean when you said that's why she took me?" When he didn't answer right away, I said: "Tanya told me the Shepherd thinks she's a patron of the arts."

He gestured at the bed. "Grab a seat. Mrs. Shepherd picks up young people she's decided have talent. In her own warped, semicrazy way, she thinks she's doing us a favor. She's giving us time. Support. Whatever. She's grooming us."

"But what's the point of that, if she isn't going to let us go?"

"It's for her pleasure, mostly. And she thinks devoting all our time to our, quote, art is all the fulfillment we need in our lives. As I've said already, the lady is semicrazy. But for me . . ." He stabbed a finger at the papers on his desk. "My father saw a professional baseball career ahead of me. He'd driven me toward that since he first gave me a baseball on my third birthday. He was a failed player himself when he was young. Unfortunately for me, I turned out to be good. So there was no escape. My mom . . ." He stroked his small wisp of a beard. "My mom was from County Sligo, a storyteller. She had two poems published in a literary magazine. Editors told her she had a way with words. I inherited that. If she had lived, things might have been different for me. I don't know. She passed away when I was nine."

"But . . . how did Mrs. Shepherd find out all this? Did you tell her? Did you know her before?"

"It took awhile for me to learn what happened. In the end I got it from her. She told me how she was on a cruise once. It was after her husband died and she met my mother's sister, my aunt Lucy, and her husband, Frank. They got friendly. My aunt told the Shepherd about me. She'd never liked my dad. She said he kept my mom from using her full potential and now he was keeping me. But I think she bragged about my baseball, too. About how I was already being talked about. All this stuff about me being Mr. Versatility, how I was hitting so many home runs over the left-field fence that the girls' soccer team there had to start wearing helmets."

He gave another wide loop of a smile. "Sorry, girls. Aunt Lucy went on about how passionate I was with my writing, how I'd like to spend every minute on that, but my father . . ." He spread out his hands. "My aunt Lucy always did gab too much. Anyway, when the Shepherd got home, she started clipping columns about me from the papers. She has a scrapbook. She showed me. Of course the book's so big for me now that I had to stand on it to read it. All this stuff. 'Is he a better pitcher or a hitter?' 'Hard to believe the ease with which McNamara Chang plays.' Nobody mentioned the pressure. Or the fact that I hated every bit of it." He tilted his chair so it balanced on the back two legs. "So she decided to rescue me. She decided to rescue Tanya, too. And John."

"She's rescuing us? By turning us into freaks? By locking us into this—this weirdo life? What made her think I needed to be rescued?"

"She has some reason," Mac said gently. "Something she saw. Or heard. Or just thought she knew."

I took my hands away from my face and looked up at him. "And you go along with this?"

"What else is there to do?" he asked.

"And you're okay?"

"Sort of," he said. "As long as I stay inside my book."

"What about the rest of us? We don't have books to stay inside. We want to get out of here, to go home." My voice was rising. "You're the oldest. You should be helping us."

He didn't answer. I watched as he picked up a silvery mechanical pencil and tapped it on his desk. "I think she bought this pencil as part of a small set. It would be uncomfortable to write with if my hand was its normal size, but for now it's just right."

He wasn't going to answer.

"She brings me leads. She does think of helpful things like that."

"Great!" I muttered. "Real helpful."

His face creased in a frown. "John wanted to take my pencil once and use it as a lever for some plan he thought he had. But I wouldn't give it up. He and Tanya were furious with me. But the plan wouldn't have worked anyway. And Mrs. Shepherd might have taken away my pencil. Or it might have snapped in two. Tanya grumbled that it should always be the most good for the most people. She's never forgiven me for that. Or for not joining in all of the futile escape plans she and John cooked up. I'll try anything—anything that has an earthly chance."

The slim wand of metal that he was holding shone in the lamplight.

Mac might not want to give it up, but I could steal it. It could be a weapon.

Mac was looking at me. "Don't even think what you're thinking. There's no way you're going to get it from me."

I took a deep breath. We'd see about that.

"What's the title of your book?" I asked. "Book Two?"

"The Kingdom of Cuchulainn and the Second She-

Demon," he said and the frown was gone.

I nodded. "Sounds interesting."

He nodded back, with a tilt of his head that let me know our conversation was over.

I had to go.

I got a glass of warm juice in the kitchen, postponing the moment when I'd have to go into the room that was to be mine. A calendar lay on the kitchen countertop, regular size, probably, but monstrously big to me. The large print across the top said AMERICANA, and the picture for June showed a scene of Beetlehawk Harbor. Whether that was a real place or an imaginary one, I didn't know. It showed a colonial house with an old-fashioned horse and buggy in front, a river scattered with boulders, a sign on a store that said CLAMS AND OYSTERS, three women in period clothing, a bait shop, a sky filled with clouds, a cherry tree dripping pink and white blossoms, in the background, a slice of ocean.

I looked at it closely. Fake. Bogus. Not even well done.

But still. My chest hurt and I could feel the start of tears. Would I ever again see a real ocean, a real river, a cherry tree in bloom?

I looked at the squares. Mrs. Shepherd had filled them in.

On Tuesday, June tenth was printed *John—dinner*. There was a line through *John* and *Kyle* was printed above it. The next square, the eleventh, said *Mac—walk, Tanya—dinner*. The twelfth was *John/Kyle—walk, Lulu—dinner*. All the way through the month we were rotated for dinners and walks. I flipped the page to July, and it was filled in, too. August, September, all the way to December thirty-first. In every John square, his name was canceled and mine penciled in on top. December thirty-first. John slash Kyle.

Our lives organized.

New Year's Eve with Mrs. Shepherd!

The lukewarm juice was making me sick again. I set it into the sink and then emptied it and watched it trickle slowly down the small drain.

Plumbing by Magnus the Magnificent.

There wasn't a sound anywhere as I went into the room that had been John's and that was now to be mine for night, after night, after awful night.

CHAPTER 10

I looked at the brushes and canvases and tubes of paint, but I looked at a distance. Not yet. Maybe not ever.

The room had a golden glow in the light that spilled from the yellow lamp shade. Almost like fake sunshine.

There was a dresser, and I went straight to it. The three drawers held jeans and sweaters and T-shirts, most still in their cardboard-backed, shrink-wrapped packets from some toy store. There was Victor's or Brian's beach outfit, striped shirt, red swim trunks, even a beach ball. Victor or Brian was ready for every occasion. He could go skiing in a heavy jacket and ski pants with a perky cap and

remember. I thought about the guy with the
who sometimes came in. No, that wasn't it.
Dalton with his guitar. No. The woman . . .
t straight up in bed.

e woman with the hat and the sunglasses and
p of bright red hair that had come loose on the
er face. I notice faces. I think about how to
hem. I remembered thinking the woman didn't
in Jumpin' Juice. It was a kid's hangout.

y back down in the doll's bed. That face, the
n it coarse, the eyes too bulgy behind the
s. That wisp of impossibly red hair.

umbled on the table by the bed and found
stone.

at's where I'd seen the Shepherd before!

ied to remember what Jason and I'd been talk-
out, sitting at the counter in Jumpin' Juice
ay. I squeezed my eyes tight shut. I'd been
him how I wouldn't be able to keep on with
classes. It was too hard for Mom. "Twenty
a lesson," I'd said. "That's a lot of money for
om to fork out."

eah, but you're so good." I could almost hear
s voice saying that.

lle had leaned across the counter. I remembered

mittens or lounge in a dark blue robe piped in scarlet. There was an empty packet that said VICTOR'S SECRETS, an imitation of Victoria's Secret, the lingerie chain that advertised all over. I looked at the six elastic fasteners that had probably held underwear that John had had to use, whether he liked it or not, and I had this stupid thought: *And what am I supposed to do? No underwear.*

But the bottom drawer held shorts and T-shirts that he must have worn and that had been laundered and put away. I closed the drawer. It would be horrible having to wear those, knowing about John and how he'd died.

But I'd have to. Already my cargo pants and the white shirt I'd put on two days ago were dirty. And I suspected I didn't smell so good.

I got undressed and hung my clothes over the wooden chair, the same kind of chair that I had sat on at Mrs. Shepherd's table, that John had used to rush at her. A Magnus-made chair. Then I opened the drawer again. No use being picky, not if I was going to be here for a while. A little while.

I pulled out a pair of khakis and put them on. They fit. Well, John was only a bit taller than me, according to the marks on the kitchen door. And we must both be about the same height as Victor and Brian. That would be about eight inches on a ruler. The inside of the left pocket was crumpled. I put my hand in and felt something in the corner. It was a round stone, white, no bigger than a large pea that must have been in there and shrunk down with him. In real life it might have been the size of a Ping-Pong ball. Something was scratched on it, so small now I could scarcely see it. I held it up to the light and saw an angel, a flying angel, with her wings laid back. An angel! It was as if John had sent me a message, a guardian angel to keep me safe. I rubbed my finger across it. But it hadn't kept John safe.

I went over to the bed, the stone cool in my hand. It was a single bed, doll-sized for a doll-sized guy. I didn't want to get into it.

I lay on top of the red chenille cover, staring wide-eyed at the ceiling. When I turned my head I could see the wall with the faded paint where the postcard of Caruso had hung. My heart was fluttering, weak as a dying bird's wings. I tried to stay awake in case Mrs. Shepherd would come, put in her big hand, grab me from where I lay, take me up to her kingdom, not the kingdom of the angels, but the kingdom of the she-demon.

But I drifted into an exh___ jumble of pictures that mad___ shivering with cold, John's st___ I put it on the small table by t___ still spilling its sunshine. I gu___ would always be sunny in he___ covers. There was a blanket ___ square cut from a standard ___ was coarse-weave linen. Initi___ one corner. M.K.S. Magnus K___ one of his handkerchiefs.

I lay in the dark, sleep go___ pening at home? Were the p___ mother making one of thos___ TV? I turned my face into th___ to think about her. And wha___ On my art-class days we'd m___ he'd ride with me partwa___ Jumpin' Juice for a smoothie. ___ is in high school. She dates ___ she'd always give us a top-___ Jason and I'd talk.

Something about Jumpin'___ Something important.

I lay in the doll's bed, m___

her lipstick, raspberry pink, and her diamond nose ring winking in the sun. "You're a wonderful artist, Kyle. Everybody says."

All at once I'd had the feeling that someone was watching me, and I'd glanced at the woman. Her eyes glittered behind her glasses, and they were looking right at me.

I remembered how uncomfortable that had made me feel.

Everything was coming back to me about that day, every word, every glance. I gnawed at the edge of the sheet.

She knew I rode home the same way two nights of the week along the dark and deserted Anney's Road. She'd taken me.

Okay, Kyle, I told myself. *Think through the panic inside your head. Think!*

Mac was a writer. She'd taken him.

John had been a singer, good enough to get that partial scholarship he hadn't been able to take.

Tanya? She'd been kidnapped like the rest of us, though I didn't exactly know why. She was a disappointment to the Shepherd.

I wanted to be an artist. She'd heard me say it. She'd heard me say I'd have to stop my classes.

Maybe she even knew that someone had paid a hundred bucks for one of my paintings and she'd thought I must be pretty good and that it would be a shame if I had to give it up.

What about Lulu, a four-year-old kid? What did the Shepherd want with her?

"She's teaching me to be Shirley Temple," Lulu had told me, delight in her voice.

The dog? Who was she teaching Pippy to be? Lassie?

I heard my own raggedy breathing. The Shepherd was totally crazy, insane. We were being held prisoner by a madwoman.

I was wakened by the house shaking. The roof was lifting, and then I heard her cheery boom of a voice and saw her monstrous, smiling face right above me. Her head filled the entire space where the roof had been.

It was morning. I knuckled the sleep from my eyes, but for a few seconds I thought I was still dreaming. I blinked and got up on one elbow. Gray light oozed in from somewhere.

"Oh, Kyle! What a slugabug," she was saying brightly.

I cowered down in the bed and pulled the M.K.S. handkerchief up to my chin. The hard lump under my back was John's stone. I wriggled it out and closed my hand around it.

"Good morning, Tanya. Good morning, Mac. Hard at work already? I can't wait to hear what happened to the druids at the winter solstice. Remember, you'll be walking with me later and we can talk. We'll take Pippy, too. She's putting on too much weight. I see Lulu's still asleep, my little sweetie." She smiled a huge, red-lipsticked smile.

"Well, here's breakfast. Oatmeal, you should eat it while it's hot. I heated the milk for you, too. Orange juice. And this nice bread."

Each time she spoke, I saw her hand in the glove come down into the house and probably set the food on the floor of the kitchen, out of my range of sight.

"Kyle!" The big, grotesque eyes were looking at me. They were bloodshot this morning, laced with red spiderwebs. "I hope you slept well?" she asked. "Were you warm enough?"

I didn't know how I got out of the bed and across the floor so quickly. I grabbed the closest tube of paint and threw it at her face with all the strength I could pull together, grabbed the second, the third, and pitched them, too. They were heavy, but I didn't feel their weight.

I'd done no good.

She fended off the first one with her gloved hand, and it dropped back inside the house. She ducked, and the second and the third disappeared into the space where her face had been. I stood poised, another tube at the ready, but her face didn't reappear.

What was that? That sudden awful sound?

It was a jungle noise, a lion's cough, a baboon's grunt, so terrifying I dropped to the floor on all fours, my arms around my head.

"Tanya! Tanya!" Lulu screamed. "She's growling. I'm so scared of her when she growls."

I peered up. Tanya had Lulu pressed against her. "It's okay, sweetie. It doesn't last long. Remember?"

Mac was in the room, crouching beside me.

"You shouldn't infuriate her like that," he whispered. "It's not worth it."

There was a loud boom, and another.

The house moved. Tanya and Lulu lost their balance and tumbled down beside us.

Pippy whimpered.

"She's kicking the wall," Mac shouted.

Now there was a silence that was almost worse than the noise. What was she was doing out there? Was she standing, her hands raised to pick the house up and throw it against the wall, the way she'd thrown John? No. It would be too heavy. Was she going to pick me up and throw me?

I heard shuffling, and her face was back in the roof space. One of her eyes twitched.

"You could have hurt me quite seriously, Kyle." Calm voice. Small smile. "For now I'll . . ." Her voice grew fainter as the lid went back on the house and the clips clicked into place.

Mac stood up, holding the one tube of paint that had fallen back into the house. "Looks like you lost the others," he said shakily.

Tanya clapped weakly. "I'm really proud of you, Kyle," she said. "At least you tried." She stayed on the floor, her arms around Lulu. "All over," she murmured. "All over now."

"Does she . . . growl like that often?" I asked. "It sounded like a beast outside there."

"That's what she is, all right," Tanya said. "That's her anger growl. It's also her frustration growl. We never get used to it. Sometimes there's a follow-up. Sometimes not. You were lucky."

Mac placed the paint tube next to the others, lining them in a neat row. "She might take them all from you if you're not careful," he muttered. "You never know with her. She hates to be thwarted."

"What does that word mean, Tanya?" Lulu sobbed. "I don't want to do it."

"It just means Mrs. Shepherd doesn't ever want us to go against her," Tanya said.

I took a deep breath. "I don't care. I'll thwart her every way I can. I don't give a damn."

"But you will," Mac said.

mittens or lounge in a dark blue robe piped in scarlet. There was an empty packet that said VICTOR'S SECRETS, an imitation of Victoria's Secret, the lingerie chain that advertised all over. I looked at the six elastic fasteners that had probably held underwear that John had had to use, whether he liked it or not, and I had this stupid thought: *And what am I supposed to do? No underwear.*

But the bottom drawer held shorts and T-shirts that he must have worn and that had been laundered and put away. I closed the drawer. It would be horrible having to wear those, knowing about John and how he'd died.

But I'd have to. Already my cargo pants and the white shirt I'd put on two days ago were dirty. And I suspected I didn't smell so good.

I got undressed and hung my clothes over the wooden chair, the same kind of chair that I had sat on at Mrs. Shepherd's table, that John had used to rush at her. A Magnus-made chair. Then I opened the drawer again. No use being picky, not if I was going to be here for a while. A little while.

I pulled out a pair of khakis and put them on. They fit. Well, John was only a bit taller than me, according to the marks on the kitchen door. And we must both be about the same height as Victor and Brian. That would be about eight inches on a ruler. The inside of the left pocket was crumpled. I put my hand in and felt something in the corner. It was a round stone, white, no bigger than a large pea that must have been in there and shrunk down with him. In real life it might have been the size of a Ping-Pong ball. Something was scratched on it, so small now I could scarcely see it. I held it up to the light and saw an angel, a flying angel, with her wings laid back. An angel! It was as if John had sent me a message, a guardian angel to keep me safe. I rubbed my finger across it. But it hadn't kept John safe.

I went over to the bed, the stone cool in my hand. It was a single bed, doll-sized for a doll-sized guy. I didn't want to get into it.

I lay on top of the red chenille cover, staring wide-eyed at the ceiling. When I turned my head I could see the wall with the faded paint where the postcard of Caruso had hung. My heart was fluttering, weak as a dying bird's wings. I tried to stay awake in case Mrs. Shepherd would come, put in her big hand, grab me from where I lay, take me up to her kingdom, not the kingdom of the angels, but the kingdom of the she-demon.

But I drifted into an exhausted sleep, dreamed in a jumble of pictures that made no sense, and woke up, shivering with cold, John's stone clenched in my hand. I put it on the small table by the bed. The lamplight was still spilling its sunshine. I guessed that, day or night, it would always be sunny in here. I scrambled under the covers. There was a blanket, unhemmed, probably a square cut from a standard-sized blanket. The sheet was coarse-weave linen. Initials were embroidered in one corner. M.K.S. Magnus Kroener Shepherd. It was one of his handkerchiefs.

I lay in the dark, sleep gone now. What was happening at home? Were the police searching? Was my mother making one of those heartrending pleas on TV? I turned my face into the pillow. I couldn't bear to think about her. And what about my friend Jason? On my art-class days we'd meet at the bike rack and he'd ride with me partway. Then we'd stop at Jumpin' Juice for a smoothie. Belle, the counter girl, is in high school. She dates Jason's big brother and she'd always give us a top-off without us asking. Jason and I'd talk.

Something about Jumpin' Juice was bugging me. Something important.

I lay in the doll's bed, muddled, but knowing I

89

had to remember. I thought about the guy with the beard who sometimes came in. No, that wasn't it. Jimmy Dalton with his guitar. No. The woman . . .

I sat straight up in bed.

The woman with the hat and the sunglasses and the wisp of bright red hair that had come loose on the side. Her face. I notice faces. I think about how to draw them. I remembered thinking the woman didn't belong in Jumpin' Juice. It was a kid's hangout.

I lay back down in the doll's bed. That face, the skin on it coarse, the eyes too bulgy behind the glasses. That wisp of impossibly red hair.

I fumbled on the table by the bed and found John's stone.

That's where I'd seen the Shepherd before!

I tried to remember what Jason and I'd been talking about, sitting at the counter in Jumpin' Juice that day. I squeezed my eyes tight shut. I'd been telling him how I wouldn't be able to keep on with my art classes. It was too hard for Mom. "Twenty bucks a lesson," I'd said. "That's a lot of money for my mom to fork out."

"Yeah, but you're so good." I could almost hear Jason's voice saying that.

Belle had leaned across the counter. I remembered

her lipstick, raspberry pink, and her diamond nose ring winking in the sun. "You're a wonderful artist, Kyle. Everybody says."

All at once I'd had the feeling that someone was watching me, and I'd glanced at the woman. Her eyes glittered behind her glasses, and they were looking right at me.

I remembered how uncomfortable that had made me feel.

Everything was coming back to me about that day, every word, every glance. I gnawed at the edge of the sheet.

She knew I rode home the same way two nights of the week along the dark and deserted Anney's Road. She'd taken me.

Okay, Kyle, I told myself. *Think through the panic inside your head. Think!*

Mac was a writer. She'd taken him.

John had been a singer, good enough to get that partial scholarship he hadn't been able to take.

Tanya? She'd been kidnapped like the rest of us, though I didn't exactly know why. She was a disappointment to the Shepherd.

I wanted to be an artist. She'd heard me say it. She'd heard me say I'd have to stop my classes.

Maybe she even knew that someone had paid a hundred bucks for one of my paintings and she'd thought I must be pretty good and that it would be a shame if I had to give it up.

What about Lulu, a four-year-old kid? What did the Shepherd want with her?

"She's teaching me to be Shirley Temple," Lulu had told me, delight in her voice.

The dog? Who was she teaching Pippy to be? Lassie?

I heard my own raggedy breathing. The Shepherd was totally crazy, insane. We were being held prisoner by a madwoman.

I was wakened by the house shaking. The roof was lifting, and then I heard her cheery boom of a voice and saw her monstrous, smiling face right above me. Her head filled the entire space where the roof had been.

It was morning. I knuckled the sleep from my eyes, but for a few seconds I thought I was still dreaming. I blinked and got up on one elbow. Gray light oozed in from somewhere.

"Oh, Kyle! What a slugabug," she was saying brightly.

I cowered down in the bed and pulled the M.K.S. handkerchief up to my chin. The hard lump under my back was John's stone. I wriggled it out and closed my hand around it.

"Good morning, Tanya. Good morning, Mac. Hard at work already? I can't wait to hear what happened to the druids at the winter solstice. Remember, you'll be walking with me later and we can talk. We'll take Pippy, too. She's putting on too much weight. I see Lulu's still asleep, my little sweetie." She smiled a huge, red-lipsticked smile.

"Well, here's breakfast. Oatmeal, you should eat it while it's hot. I heated the milk for you, too. Orange juice. And this nice bread."

Each time she spoke, I saw her hand in the glove come down into the house and probably set the food on the floor of the kitchen, out of my range of sight.

"Kyle!" The big, grotesque eyes were looking at me. They were bloodshot this morning, laced with red spiderwebs. "I hope you slept well?" she asked. "Were you warm enough?"

I didn't know how I got out of the bed and across the floor so quickly. I grabbed the closest tube of paint and threw it at her face with all the strength I could pull together, grabbed the second, the third, and pitched them, too. They were heavy, but I didn't feel their weight.

I'd done no good.

She fended off the first one with her gloved hand, and it dropped back inside the house. She ducked, and the second and the third disappeared into the space where her face had been. I stood poised, another tube at the ready, but her face didn't reappear.

What was that? That sudden awful sound?

It was a jungle noise, a lion's cough, a baboon's grunt, so terrifying I dropped to the floor on all fours, my arms around my head.

"Tanya! Tanya!" Lulu screamed. "She's growling. I'm so scared of her when she growls."

I peered up. Tanya had Lulu pressed against her. "It's okay, sweetie. It doesn't last long. Remember?"

Mac was in the room, crouching beside me.

"You shouldn't infuriate her like that," he whispered. "It's not worth it."

There was a loud boom, and another.

The house moved. Tanya and Lulu lost their balance and tumbled down beside us.

Pippy whimpered.

"She's kicking the wall," Mac shouted.

Now there was a silence that was almost worse than the noise. What was she was doing out there? Was she standing, her hands raised to pick the house up and throw it against the wall, the way she'd thrown John? No. It would be too heavy. Was she going to pick me up and throw me?

I heard shuffling, and her face was back in the roof space. One of her eyes twitched.

"You could have hurt me quite seriously, Kyle." Calm voice. Small smile. "For now I'll . . ." Her voice grew fainter as the lid went back on the house and the clips clicked into place.

Mac stood up, holding the one tube of paint that had fallen back into the house. "Looks like you lost the others," he said shakily.

Tanya clapped weakly. "I'm really proud of you, Kyle," she said. "At least you tried." She stayed on the floor, her arms around Lulu. "All over," she murmured. "All over now."

"Does she . . . growl like that often?" I asked. "It sounded like a beast outside there."

"That's what she is, all right," Tanya said. "That's her anger growl. It's also her frustration growl. We never get used to it. Sometimes there's a follow-up. Sometimes not. You were lucky."

Mac placed the paint tube next to the others, lining them in a neat row. "She might take them all from you if you're not careful," he muttered. "You never know with her. She hates to be thwarted."

"What does that word mean, Tanya?" Lulu sobbed. "I don't want to do it."

"It just means Mrs. Shepherd doesn't ever want us to go against her," Tanya said.

I took a deep breath. "I don't care. I'll thwart her every way I can. I don't give a damn."

"But you will," Mac said.

CHAPTER 11

I asked Mac for three pages of paper, and I made my own calendar. I copied the Shepherd's notations of the when and where for all of us. The rest of each square was to keep count of the time and of what I did. What we did. Each day was the same.

She brought our meals, and we ate together. After that we had a routine that Mac had set up.

"A routine gives shape to the day," he said. "We need that."

First we took our cold, cold showers. "Better to freeze in the morning than at night," Tanya explained.

After that we did exercises, even Lulu, stretching,

touching our toes, doing squats, sit-ups, push-ups, running in place.

Then we dusted Magnus's furniture and swept the floors and rugs. "We don't do windows," Mac told me one day, so seriously that for a minute I didn't get the joke. "We don't have windows," he added helpfully. It was no joke.

The house shone. We hated it, but we had to live in it. Keeping busy, moving, helped us stay sane.

Sometimes, though, I did freak out. I'd feel the house closing in on me, and I couldn't breathe. It was smothering, and I wanted to scream. Once Tanya did scream. She banged her head against the wall, then sank down on the floor, sobbing and sobbing. It frightened Lulu, who began to cry, too, and Tanya got up and went to her and wiped her eyes.

"Silly Tanya was just a bit upset," she explained, cuddling Lulu close. "Not to worry."

She never broke down again. At least not where we could see.

I had enough sense left to know that if we did lose it, we'd be in worse shape.

Every afternoon the three of us played cards or worked on jigsaw after jigsaw. Cats and kittens. Snow White and the dwarfs.

"They're little, like us," Lulu said. "Only we're littler."

We played word games and number games to keep our brains from rusting. To keep us from thinking hopeless thoughts. Lulu learned to count to twenty and knew her alphabet. She could recite "Jack and Jill" and "Mary Had a Little Lamb."

Tanya and I remembered movies we'd seen and changed the endings.

But most of all we wondered what was happening in the world.

Mac was hardly ever around. He had his own sure way of keeping his mind busy. I envied him a little, but I was also mad at him, too. Why couldn't he at least try to be one of us?

One day, while Lulu was napping, Tanya told me how the Shepherd got her, and I was strangely honored. It was as if she had finally decided to let me into her life.

"I just went with her willingly," Tanya said. "I was playing my violin on the street. I'd seen her for three days in a row, sitting on a bench, listening. She always put more money in my cap than anybody else."

"Where was this?" I asked.

"Santa Cruz, downtown. Ever been there?"

I nodded. "Nice."

"On the third day she asked if she could buy me a meal." Tanya looked at me with those dark, almond-shaped eyes. "A meal! Of course I went. I hadn't had a decent meal in days. Not since I ran away from the Straws."

"The who?"

"My foster parents. Third set."

I wanted to ask more, but she was suddenly quiet, plunging her hands deep in the pockets of her Betsy or Britney tartan shorts, tracing something on the blue-and-red rug with one bare foot. Then she said, "It was cold, the way it gets in Santa Cruz when the sun goes down. The Shepherd told me she had an extra jacket in the trunk of her car and so I opened the trunk and leaned in to get it and—ping." She gave me a bitter smile. "You know what happened next."

"I'm sorry," I muttered. What could I say?

"Sure," Tanya said. "I'm sorry for all of us."

Mac gave me four pieces of paper and reluctantly let me use his pencil. I sketched the four of us, and we exchanged them with one another. I took Tanya's.

"Keepsakes," I told them. "For when we get out."

My words were brave, but sometimes, in private, I thought we never would.

There were nights when Lulu danced for us while Tanya sang "On the Good Ship Lollipop." Her curls bobbed, and her tiny feet tapped on the wooden floor.

"Mrs. Shepherd shows me videos of Shirley," she told us. "Shirley's so pretty."

"You are, too, Lulu," I said. "Pretty as a possum."

It was easy to make Lulu giggle, even here.

In all that time I did not touch the Shepherd's brushes or paints.

I kept John's stone with me, always.

Every night I checked my calendar. Time was passing. I worried about my mother. By now she'd probably decided I was dead. There'd be no hope left.

I tried to keep mine alive.

Each week the Shepherd gave us our vitamin shots. Each week Lulu cried. "I don't want to be stuck. Please no, Mrs. Shepherd. Please no!" And the Shepherd would soothe, "Don't be frightened, little one. It's for your own good."

Huddled below in the living room, waiting for our turn, we'd hear.

"Liar!" Tanya would hiss.

The Shepherd took us on our walks, one of us every day.

One morning I raced ahead of her and then ran around and around her feet, leashing them together, hoping she would fall. I jammed myself against her giant-sized Nike walking shoe with all my weight. She fell, but not hard enough. She simply sat up, leaned over, and unwound herself by whirling me around on my end of the leash, untwisting me till I was dizzy.

I stood, swaying, waiting for that terrifying growl, but she only brushed the loose dirt and leaves off her jeans and said mildly, "I thought you were enjoying our walk."

She seemed almost amused. Mac was right. You never knew about her. The word was unpredictable.

I hurt all over. Rage flared in me. "Someday you won't find us so funny," I said, and she looked at me in bogus astonishment.

"What are you talking about, Kyle?"

At dinners she'd chat constantly, asking me about my painting, telling me how much she was looking forward to having art up on all the bare walls of the dollhouse. "Those walls have been waiting just for you, Kyle." Her loving voice made my stomach heave.

"I'm not painting for you, ever," I told her.

"Be careful how you speak to me, young man!" she snapped. "My tolerance only goes so far." The loving voice and the loving look were gone, and I was instantly afraid. I looked up at her and saw the huge, gloved hand hovering over me, and there was that awful rumble starting, the forecast of the growl. I hunched my shoulders up to my ears, and my mind went blank. She was going to whack me, smash me till I was a smear on the ground.

The growl died to a vibration, somewhere in her throat.

I heard her take in a great swoosh of breath then, and her hand dropped to her side.

My legs were so weak, I had trouble walking, and she smiled down at me, that tender, loving, scarlet smile. "Would you like me to carry you, Kyle?"

"No, thanks," I said, weakly but very politely.

Oh, yes, I needed to be careful what I said to her. Or I'd be dead.

Each time we walked, I scoped out the surroundings. I could see the roof of a house way, way across a raggedy field. There was a narrow dirt road that ran alongside the field and up to the doors of the wooden garage. The Buick would be inside there.

The four of us knew that Buick's dark, dangerous trunk. Her house was set back among trees. Vines twined against its walls. Looking at them, I thought of Jack and the Beanstalk. You could climb up one of these if you were Jack's size, or mine, and the giant would be waiting. *Fee, fi, fo, fum.*

We walked on a broken path through her garden that was overgrown and filled with weeds twice as tall as I was. It was strange to see a puff of a dandelion in seed, exactly at my level. I'd never realized how beautiful and delicate each little seed was. I saw ladybugs the way I'd never seen them before. I saw worms, big as pink, ringed snakes. Sometimes I felt I was looking through a microscope.

Usually she took Pippy with us. He was the only one allowed to run free. He liked it when I raced ahead as far as the leash would let me. He liked chasing me and jumping on me.

I stared at the field. *Four people could hide among those weeds and tasseled grasses*, I thought.

And she'd never find us.

The walks were more bearable than the dinners. The Shepherd played jazz for me, thinking it was my kind of music. What she didn't realize was that hearing my mother's CDs made my throat choke with tears and made me all the more determined to escape. Sometimes we had Aretha Franklin singing for us or Billie Holiday or Ella Fitzgerald. They were not all our CDs. These she bought especially for me. She cocked her head and smiled at me fondly. "Is there anyone else you'd like to hear? Another CD? It would be no trouble to get it for you."

I wouldn't answer.

I asked Tanya what kind of music the Shepherd played for her. Tanya shrugged. "Violin solos. She likes to put on Dvořák, the melody of the third movement of his string quartet. The one in F major." Her voice broke. "She watches me. I don't know if she's hoping for thanks or tears. I don't give her either. It nearly destroyed her when my violin didn't come down with me. And I'm glad about it, even though I may never play it again." She'd hidden her eyes with her hand and I thought she was crying. But when she looked up I saw the hardness in her.

"She lets me visit it. You've seen it there, on the chair in the corner of the dining room? She opens the case and says I can touch it. She says I can pluck the strings if I want. I don't move or answer. She gets nothing from me, ever." Tanya buried her fingers in her hair. "Here I am, living in Magnus's house, taking up one of her precious rooms. And the only way she can get rid of me is to . . . well, get rid of me."

"You mean, kill you?" I had trouble getting the words out, and I thought immediately of that monstrous gloved hand that had hovered above me. Easy enough to kill any one of us.

Tanya smiled at me. "Well, she can't very well set me free."

I felt close to Tanya. We were together all day, every day, except for the times we had to spend with the Shepherd. I was thinking about her too much, and I tried not to. But the trying only seemed to make me think about her more.

CHAPTER 12

On Mondays, early, the

Shepherd picked up our laundry. We put it in a mesh bag, and she took it and brought the clothes back clean and folded.

When the mesh bag went up on Monday, September eighth, I went up inside it.

We'd planned it for days. Who would go? I'd argued that it was my idea, so I should be the one.

"I'm the smallest, except for Lulu. And I'm black and less noticeable," Tanya said. "It should be me."

Mac shook his head. "It's not going to work anyway. She's too smart."

Tanya glared at him. "You don't have to go. We

know you're fine with staying here."

There was no expression on Mac's face. "I'm just saying it's not a good idea."

Tanya gave him an unfriendly look. "You never think anything we try is a good idea."

"Well, nothing *has* been, so far," Mac said.

"It would be nice if you'd be positive for once," Tanya said. "If not for us, for Lulu."

In the end, the three of us drew al dente spaghetti strings to see which one of us it would be.

"You're sure you want to be in on this, Mac?" I'd asked, and he'd nodded without really answering. "Longest string gets to be it," I said.

I picked the longest one.

And today was the day.

I got in, wrapped myself in Magnus's handkerchief sheet, and hid among the other laundry. So she wouldn't look for me and find me missing when she came for the bag, we'd planned two diversions. I'd be supposedly in bed, supposedly asleep. Old Bear was in my bed instead, well covered with a blanket.

"Kyle's asleep," Tanya would say if the Shepherd asked. But we hoped she wouldn't notice because of the other diversion. The other diversion was Lulu.

We'd coached her carefully. But she was only four years old and we couldn't be sure she exactly understood.

"Here's what we need you to do," Tanya said, sitting face-to-face with Lulu on the couch.

Lulu nodded solemnly.

"We're going to help Kyle get out so he can go tell someone we're here. So we won't have to stay with Mrs. Shepherd anymore."

Lulu put her thumb in her mouth, took it out again, and asked: "But can I come back and visit her sometimes? And see her Shirley Temple videos?"

Tanya swallowed hard. "If you want to," she said. "But you'll be with your mama again. And that will be good, won't it?"

Lulu smiled so her dimples flicked out and in. "That will be really good."

"So. Kyle's going to hide in the laundry bag, and then, when the Shepherd pulls him up, we want you to do a very important job for us."

"Okay," Lulu said.

"You know how Kyle taught you to do an almost cartwheel."

Lulu nodded.

"You're really good at it."

She nodded again.

"Okay, here's the plan." Tanya lowered her voice to a whisper. "And it's a secret. We don't want you to tell anybody. Not even Old Bear. Not even Pippy. And most of all, not Mrs. Shepherd. We want to surprise her."

Lulu giggled. "Pippy's listening."

I put my hands over the dog's ears, and Lulu giggled again.

"First Kyle will hide in the bag."

"Like hide-and-seek?" Lulu asked, bright eyed.

"Yes. Except we hope nobody's going to find him. Then Mrs. Shepherd will come for the laundry, the way she always does, and she'll lift off the roof, and when she does that, you watch me. I'll give you a little signal, like this." Tanya made a little salute. "Doesn't Shirley salute like this in those videos?"

Lulu clapped her hands. "She does. Just like that."

"You be watching for it. And when you see it,

you call out to Mrs. Shepherd, 'Look at me, Mrs. Shepherd. See what I can do.' Do you think you can remember that, Lulu? Can you say it back to me?"

"'Look at me, Mrs. Shepherd. See what I can do,'" Lulu repeated.

Tanya said, "That's great. That's perfect. And as soon as you've said it, you do your wonderful cartwheel, over there, by the wall. She'll be so excited to see it."

Lulu frowned. "What if I don't do a good one?"

"It's okay if you don't. Then you just try another one." Tanya paused. "You'll be playacting. Like Shirley does in her movies. Do you think you can?"

"Sure," Lulu said with a big smile.

We practiced with her over and over. I was saying her lines in my sleep. So much depended on her keeping Mrs. Shepherd's attention on her and not on the bag, and certainly not on my bed. Old Bear was way bigger than I was. But under the carefully mussed-up covers, he could pass, if she didn't look too closely.

On Sunday night, the night before I was to go, Mac and Tanya and I sat in the living room, going over every eventuality we could think of. First, of course, I could be caught before I ever got started. She could find me in the bag. Or she could see me when she tossed out the clothes, either into a hamper or directly into the washer.

"I don't think she'll even open the bag," I said. "I think the whole thing will go in. My mom had a bag like that where she put my socks when she washed them. Because one was always getting lost. It's because the socks are small and they get sucked into the pipes. Think how much smaller our clothes are."

Tanya took a deep, shuddery breath. "You know what, Kyle? I don't think you should try this. I honestly don't."

"Wait a sec," I began. "It's all planned. We're not going to abandon—"

She interrupted. "What if you're in the bag, in the washer, and the water's coming in, and you can't get out and . . . ?"

"I'll get out. You're going to tie the top string really loosely."

"She could tighten it."

"So? I can still get it open. You know we've checked to make sure my fingers go through the mesh. That's not a worry." I didn't say about a worry

I did have. Suppose I couldn't push open the lid of the washer?

"What if the bag gets tangled, and the agitator starts and . . . what if *you* get sucked into the pipes?"

"You know what *I* think," Mac said. "But you and Tanya seem to believe it can be done, so . . ." He spread his hands.

Tanya went on as if she hadn't heard him. "You won't have very long, Kyle. She'll come to take Mac on his walk." She looked at her watch that had probably been John's. "She'll be back in about two hours."

"She'll figure out you've gone and start searching," Mac said.

"But she'll check the basement first," I told him, hearing my voice, surer than I felt. "By that time I'll be safe in those weeds. On my way to that house way across the fields." I gave a quiet bogus laugh. "Think how they'll freak out when they see *little ole me*!"

Tanya's head drooped. "Waiting here is going to be so hard." I heard her sob, and I got up and sat beside her and put a brotherly arm around her. Did she think it was brotherly? I gave her a light squeeze. "We have to try, Tanya. Anything's worth the risk."

She lifted her tearstained face to mine. "Oh, no! That's what John said. You know what, Kyle? I'm beginning to think you shouldn't go. It's way too scary. Losing John was almost more than I could stand. Losing you . . ."

She left the sentence unfinished. But what she'd already said made me feel better. She'd let me know that I was important to her, too.

Monday, September eighth, came, and I went.

CHAPTER 13

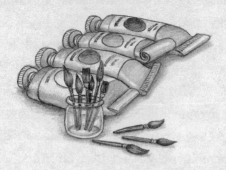

I hung in the mesh bag,

swaying gently, between the open roof and the floor of the dollhouse. I knew the Shepherd was watching Lulu's almost cartwheel.

"That's wonderful, Lulu." There was affection in her voice.

I didn't try to see what was happening, but I could guess. Lulu was speaking to Tanya. "Did I do good, Tanya? Did I say it right?"

For a moment I thought we were finished before we started. I thought the Shepherd would ask, "Say what?" in that inquisitive way of hers. But then I heard Tanya go over to Lulu and probably scoop her up before she could say anything else.

"You were perfect," Tanya said. And then, "She's been practicing Shirley Temple lines, Mrs. Shepherd. She's very good."

I imagined the Shepherd's pleased smile. "We'll watch some more of the video tomorrow, darling Lulu."

"Oh, by the way, Mrs. Shepherd," Tanya said casually. "I put Lulu's quilt and mine in the bag. They're both grubby. Sorry it's a bit heavy."

"That's perfectly okay," the Shepherd said sunnily. She'd be overwhelmed that Tanya was speaking so politely to her.

"I'm fixing chili for lunch," she called. "And I'll be back at eleven, Mac, to take you for our walk."

She dumped the bag of laundry on the basement floor while she clipped on the roof. The jolt as the bag fell took my breath away, even though I was well padded.

She swung the bag some more as she went up the steps, humming under her breath like a happy, buzzing bee.

I was curled up so tight inside the handkerchief that my legs and back were one big ache. John's stone was pushed deep in the pocket of my black shorts. We'd chosen black shorts and a dirt-colored

116

T-shirt for me "to travel in," as Mac said. They'd be camouflage when I reached the escape field. My Adidas that I'd been wearing when she took me were grimy from our walks. They weren't white anymore.

Her footsteps tapped across a floor and the bag and I swung in time with her strides. I guessed we were in her kitchen. Then there was a different underfoot sound and the bag was dumped once more on a hard, unyielding surface. I heard a *click, click*. The sound of a washer being turned on. My heart hammered so hard, I thought I might choke. What if I was wrong and she opened the bag and spilled the contents into the machine? What if she saw me, a boy shape in black shorts and T-shirt, legs scissoring down into the water? Well, she'd fish me out, probably with her trusty butterfly net. And that way at least I wouldn't drown. But another gate to escape would be closed forever.

I lay in the bag on the floor. Beside me water trickled. She was filling the machine, still humming.

And then the bag was lifted and tossed in.

I was in an echo chamber. A waterfall trickled behind me. The sound drummed in my ears. I could hear nothing else. I pushed aside the handkerchief sheet and the towels and T-shirts that were bunched around me and peered out. The gray enamel drum was close to my eyes. When I looked up, I saw the open lid of the washer, the ceiling above it, and a round bowl of a light fixture with dark speckles of dead flies inside. No Mrs. Shepherd. But no time to waste.

Hurry! Hurry!

Had she gone for more laundry? Surely she wouldn't wash just this small load. I poked at the mesh, found the top where the knot was, and pushed my fingers through. The clothes in the bag were getting wet now, soggy beneath me. Water cascaded gently on my left shoulder.

Hurry, hurry, before she comes back!

I found the loose knot that Tanya had tied. It had tightened now with the swinging of the bag, but it was still dry. It would be tighter when it got wet. I jabbed my fingers through, trying not to panic. If I panicked, I'd never open that knot. I was gasping, muttering, "Come on, come on," as I pried awkwardly through the netting. I had it. The top was open.

No! Oh, no! Footsteps coming back. I slipped myself quickly under one of our towels that was wet and soggy on one side. A load of clothes came down on top of me, pushing me under the water, and then a dry, gritty shower that I thought was soap powder. There was a loud, solid *bang*, and I was in complete darkness.

I fought my way up through wads of clothes, hers. I smelled her jasmine perfume, mixed with the sharp nose-tingling smell of the soap that made me sneeze and sneeze again. I pinched my nose with my thumb and finger. She couldn't hear, could she? I was suffocating, smothering, the sound of the dripping water trickling behind me. The clothes she'd added on top were still dry. Now I was standing on them, unsteadily, as I tried to step from one soft, yielding pile to the next, my arms windmilling for balance. My fingers brushed against something hard and slippery. The agitator. I held on and pulled myself up and onto it. Where was the water level now? If this thing started to spin and jump, I'd be tossed down into a whirlpool, a drowning trap. I stood on the breadth of the agitator and began crawling up. It was grainy with dried soap, and slippery. Up, up, up. Like being on a curving spiral path slick with ice. I stood again, raised my arms, and felt the washer lid just above my head. I caught my breath. This was it! I listened but could hear only the stream of water behind me. She must have gone. I had to get out of here. I pushed, and the lid lifted easily. I shoved hard, and it swung all the way back, jittering on its hinges, and I hoisted myself up onto the wide rim of the machine. The room—I guessed it was only for laundry—was empty.

I didn't know this room. Magnus hadn't included it in our house. There was a dryer and, beside me, a row of shelves that held soap powder and an immense bottle of bleach and spray bottles of stain remover. She stored her boxes of garbage bags here, too. The shelves were white enamel, supported on either side by white enamel poles. Below me, the washer gave a jump and a creak and the agitator began to twist. I took a deep, thankful breath, grabbed for the pole, and slid down it. My hands were wet and I slid faster than I'd imagined, landing on the tiled floor with a thump that knocked all the breath out of me. I stood, aching everywhere, dripping. A slice of pain shafted into my ankle. No time to worry about that.

I was on a tiled floor, big, square gray tiles. In front of me was an open door. Inside was another small room, not the kitchen. A bathroom. There was a sink and a toilet. There was a picture of an old-fashioned girl washing herself at a round blue-rimmed bowl. She looked shyly over her shoulder at me. There were blue hand towels on a rail. A bowl of fake blue flowers sat on the tank. Above the toilet was a smoky louvered window. And the louvers were at a slant.

I limped across the floor, leaving a trail of soapy water. Pain shot through my ankle at every step. I stared up at the white toilet seat, so far above me. How could I reach it? There had to be a way. *Come on, Kyle, think, think.* A toilet-brush holder was pushed in the corner. I dragged out the long-handled brush and wedged it between the wall and the bowl. Hand over hand I swarmed up it while the girl in the picture dimpled modestly. The seat was within reach now. I stretched and my fingers touched it, and I let go of the brush handle and grabbed its rim. I was up, hobbling around it to the window. I had to jump to reach the window ledge, hanging for a few seconds before I was able to climb up. I clambered onto the window ledge. There was a screen with a clip that almost broke my fingers as I pried it free. Below the window was the wall, and growing there was a purple-flowered vine with a thick, nubby stem. I'd seen these vines before. I'd thought then that they would be easy to climb up. *Fee, fi, fo, fum.* Or down. This was my chance.

I sat on the lowest louver and let myself slide down through the vine till a fork-shaped growth stopped me. I clutched at it with both hands and rested there for a few seconds, straddling it, breathing hard before I began the long climb the rest of the way down.

I was on the ground. The air was morning sweet, the sky blue and streaked with wisps of clouds, the smell of earth and honeysuckle so delicious my throat choked up. No leash on me. No Shepherd tugging at me, chattering in her self-satisfied voice. I could hardly believe it. It was already warm, and my wet clothes steamed gently. Across the weed-thick field I could see the roof of the house, my goal and sanctuary. I had to get moving.

I checked my watch. We'd figured on two hours before she came to get Mac. I'd already used up three-quarters of one of them. I glanced up at the house. There were windows everywhere, some of them with the vines trailing prettily around them. I'd noticed the windows on our walks, but my attention hadn't been intense, the way it was now.

She could be looking out of any one of them. And I had to cross the strip of dirt pathway before I could hide myself among the grass and weeds.

I ran, bent almost double. On the first step my ankle gave such a searing jolt of pain that I almost fell. No time to fall. No time to feel pain.

I was in the field, hidden, the weeds and grasses as tall as I was. Safe. Safe.

I began pushing my way through them. Every step was agony. What had I done? Was my ankle broken or just sprained? I clenched my teeth. Once I'd read an account in the newspaper of a man who was determined to walk solo across Antarctica pulling a sled with all his provisions. He'd stepped in an ice hole and broken his ankle, but his determination pulled him on. He'd walked more than a hundred miles with his ankle strapped tight in his boot, sucking on pain pills. I didn't have pain pills. But I didn't have to go a hundred miles either. *Come on, Kyle. Your determination is just as strong. Keep going.*

I ran in a crouch, straightening cautiously now and then to look back at the house. It sat there among the trees, peaceful and quiet in the California sun.

I touched the angel in my pocket and kept going.

The tasseled tops of the grasses, which had seemed so light and feathery, were sharp as needles, whipping against my face and my bare arms and legs. Prickles stuck to me and clung like burrs to my clothes. Flies came sniffing at the little drops of blood on my arms and legs, ordinary-sized flies, but to me they were as big as crows.

Were Mac and Tanya and Lulu checking their watches, wondering if I'd gotten away, wondering where I was? I had to make it for them as well as for myself. The roof of the house beyond the field looked as far away as when I'd started walking, but it couldn't be. I only had an hour. I had to be getting closer.

I remembered then that I should be zigzagging, though I couldn't remember why, so I cut left a little and then right again.

Somewhere a mockingbird was calling, the same notes over and over, and then . . . and then . . . someone else was calling.

"Kyle? Kyle? I know you're in there. Come back right now!"

Oh, no! How could she have discovered I'd gone so quickly? I ran faster, realizing that she could probably see the grass moving behind me or in front of me. That was the way trackers tracked, wasn't it? The Apache brave, trailing the enemy. Would it be better to freeze, the way an animal froze when the hunter was after it? I could lie down, stay flat, wait for dark.

"Kyle? There's no use hiding. I know exactly where you are."

Snip! Snip!

She was cutting the weeds as she came. My heart thumped against my ribs.

I cautiously parted the grasses in front of me just a little. And saw. She had humongous garden shears. The blades glinted sharp in the sun. They opened and closed like the beak of some giant, murderous bird.

Snip! Snip!

Needles of grass, yellow weed blossoms, clumps of dirt flew through the air.

"I'm coming, Kyle," she called.

No way to run, no place to hide.

Snip! Snip!

I curled myself small, my arms wrapped around my head, frozen in terror. I was going to be cut in two, my head slashed from the rest of me.

She was upon me. Her shadow blocked the sun. "There you are!" she said.

I think I screamed, "Don't, don't!" But I'm not sure.

And then the butterfly net dropped over me like a cage and I was flipped, lifted, and held close to her giant face. Sun turned the red of her hair into rusted rust. Sweat lay in quivering blobs on her forehead.

She didn't growl.

She didn't speak.

She smiled and carried me at arm's length back the way I had come.

I had run so far and so hard, but going back took her only seven easy steps.

In all my life I'd never felt so helpless.

CHAPTER 11

She put me back, dripping,
into the dollhouse.

Tanya and Mac and Lulu stood in the middle of
the living room, waiting for me.

The Shepherd didn't speak. She smiled a wide,
red smile, stared at each of us in turn, clipped on the
roof, and left.

"I didn't make it," I said needlessly. My teeth
chattered with cold and fear.

"We thought you wouldn't," Tanya said. "She
came and pulled the covers off Old Bear and went
away. She didn't even ask where you were. We were
desperate."

I took a limping step.

"You're hurt," Mac said. "Sit down." He probed my ankle. "I don't think it's broken. I've seen two broken ankles, had one, and it didn't feel like this. You probably sprained it and then walked on it."

"Right," I said.

He helped me to my room. Tanya brought towels, and I dried off and put on jeans and a warm sweater that I pulled from Brian's packet. I had begun to believe I knew the difference between Victor's and Brian's tastes, as if they were real people, as if they chose their own clothes. Brian liked bright colors, and this sweater was the color of an overripe pumpkin. Sometimes I wondered if I was going as crazy as the Shepherd.

I lay on the couch in my pumpkin sweater, and Tanya sponged the bites and scratches on my face. She wrapped a wet cloth around my ankle.

Pippy lay beside me, and Lulu sat on the floor and recited for me.

"I bet she went back to the laundry room to put the clothes in the dryer," Mac said. "We didn't count on that."

"And then she saw the lid of the washer open," I said. "And I guess I left a trail, right from the start. There were probably water drips on the floor leading right into that bathroom."

There was a silence. "You couldn't have done different," Mac said gruffly. "You did well. You almost pulled it off."

Tanya brought me three baby aspirins, quartered. "The Shepherd gave us some for Lulu when she had a fever. These were left over."

I swallowed them. "I'm so sorry, you guys," I muttered.

"Don't be silly," Tanya said. "You were great."

"You were brave," Lulu said. "Like Robin Hood. He was terrifically brave."

"I'm just glad you're alive," Tanya whispered.

I managed to grin. "Me, too."

"Me, too," Mac said.

The Shepherd didn't come back to take Mac on his walk.

"She's letting us stew a bit." Tanya looked at me seriously. "You know I hate her. But I sort of understand her, too. She's lonely. She's empty. We fill her life. I was lonely a lot of the time in the foster homes. I wonder if she'll bring us lunch. It's scary when you think of how much we have to depend on her."

"But if she doesn't, we'll get hungry." Lulu's lips quivered.

"She will, Lulu. Don't worry," Tanya said.

She did bring lunch, not with her usual flourish and happy talk.

"Can you believe her?" Tanya asked. "She's hurt. She's disappointed in us. She can't understand why you tried to get away. Why we don't love it here. Why we don't love *her*."

"I sort of love her," Lulu said. "But not as much as my mama."

"I know," Tanya said tenderly.

For six days I kept my foot propped up. My walks were canceled, but my dinners with the Shepherd went on as usual. We got our vitamin shots. She never mentioned my escape effort. It was as if it had never happened.

"It's called serious denial," Mac said. "Books are full of denial."

"Is yours?" I asked.

Mac grinned. "Not too much. Back in those early days the Irish were too busy sword fighting and killing to worry about who was right and who was wrong. I don't think we've changed too much since then."

"But you do have a she-demon," I said.

"Yep. And a bull called Finnbennach that has a body the color of blood and a horse's breast and a salmon's snout and—"

Lulu squirmed. "He's scary."

"Does your hero stand up to him?" Tanya asked. "I suppose you have a hero?"

"I have and he does," Mac answered without looking at her.

"See?" Tanya said. "That's the kind of hero we like. Not the wishy-washy kind who doesn't want to try—"

I interrupted. "So tell us more."

"Finnbennach is also a demon. In my story, of course, he meets the she-demon. . . . She's only in my imagination." He grinned his wide, loopy grin—a grin directed at me that left Tanya out. "I have such a good role model here I couldn't resist. The funny thing is, when I read to the Shepherd about the she-demon, she never recognizes herself."

"Full-time denial," I said.

"How come you've never read your story to us?" Tanya asked.

"I'm nervous," Mac said. "If you didn't like it, I'd know. And even if you faked it, I'd know. And I

131

don't think I could handle that. With her it doesn't matter. Besides, she always tells me it's wonderful."

Tanya rolled her eyes.

He was back to writing every day.

Tanya and I talked and talked.

We dreamed up new and impossible plans to escape. Somehow we'd get to her phone and call for help. "We'd have to stand on the number buttons and hop," Tanya said.

"We could do that," I told her.

Somehow we'd get to her car. "I'd stand on the back of the driver's seat and steer," I told her. "You'd be down by the accelerator. Mac would be on the brake. I'd shout orders."

"I'll steer and shout the orders, thank you very much," Tanya said. "Do you think Mac would be with us?"

"He definitely would," I said.

We planned that somehow we'd get the needle from her and give her a vitamin shot so she'd be as small as us, and then we'd overpower her and make our escape.

It was the "somehows" that stopped us. We were

sure we could do all those things if we could somehow get past the "somehows."

One afternoon, Tanya was putting Lulu down
for her nap and I listened to her soft, murmuring
voice.

"We'll go kite flying when we get out. First, of
course, I'll have to ask your mama's permission. You
never go with anyone, not even a pal like me, unless
you check it with your mama first."

"I know," Lulu said. "Because there can be bad
people."

"That's right. But when your mama says it's
okay, we'll go to this great place I know. There's a hill
and you can see the ocean. There's always a breeze,
and the sky has these clouds with tails on them gal-
loping across it."

Lulu whispered sleepily, "Clouds with tails? I've
never seen clouds with tails."

"You will."

"And my kite will look like a bird, right?"

"Yes."

"And yours will be a green dragon?"

"Dragon lady, that's me."

"And we'll take Old Bear. And Pippy."

"Absolutely. We won't go without them."

133

I stood outside Lulu's room and heard the affection in Tanya's voice. I opened the door.

"Can I come kite flying, too?" I asked.

"We want you to," Lulu said.

I leaned over to kiss her nose, and she looked up at me. "Do you love me, Kyle?"

"A whole big bunch."

"Do you love Tanya?"

The question was so unexpected. Beside me, Tanya made a little embarrassed movement.

"I do love Tanya," I said. I felt heat rush to my face.

"And he loves Mac and Pippy and Old Bear, too," Tanya said quickly.

"Then kiss Old Bear and Pippy, Kyle," Lulu ordered.

I did. I half waited for her to say, "And kiss Tanya," and then what?

She didn't.

And I was a bit disappointed.

My calendar squares were filling up. The Xs showed how long we'd been here. The zero on September eighth reminded me of the day I'd tried the big escape and failed. It was October now. Some of the leaves were changing color around her house. I'd been here for more than three months. My hair had grown to shoulder length.

"She'd cut it for you if you like," Tanya said. "I let her cut my nails. It's too miserable to go around with claws."

She cut my nails, too, delicately and carefully, but I refused her offer to trim my hair.

It was October sixth.

The Shepherd carried me back from dinner with her. We'd had music as usual, a Charlie Parker CD.

She was prattling away as she clattered down the basement steps, telling me about Magnus and the project he hadn't managed to finish before he passed on. Something about changing human beings in the most radical ways. I guessed maybe we were the start of that experiment.

"It's called genetic tinkering," the Shepherd said. "Embryos could be manipulated to increase their intelligence. There'd be no more low IQs. Imagine it, Kyle!"

She was so intense, the way she always was when she talked about Magnus, her voice so loud and excited that she didn't hear what I heard. There was a *drip, drip* of water, coming from somewhere close. If I hadn't tuned her out, I wouldn't have heard it either.

I peered over the top of her knuckles.

Drops of water fell from the bottom of her huge water heater. Each one looked as big as a quarter to me, but I guessed they were really pretty small.

My heart began to beat extra fast. My mind was moving extra fast, too. A leak could be big trouble for her.

And an incredible piece of luck for the Lambkins.

CHAPTER 15

"There's a leak in one of the basement pipes," I told Tanya. "A trickle of water is running across the floor. It's small now, but it will get worse. Unless she can do the plumbing herself, she'll have to bring someone down here to fix it for her."

Tanya buried her face in her hands, then looked up at me. Her voice shook. "We've never had anybody down here in all this time. Nobody but her. Could this be our chance, Kyle?"

"Are we going to be found?" Lulu asked, looking at each of us in turn. "Will we get to go home?"

"Maybe," Tanya muttered. "We'll scream and shout. The plumber might hear us."

I closed my eyes, trying to think it through. "The Shepherd will know we'll try that. She's never going to take the risk. I bet she moves us, house and all."

"No way," Tanya said. "This house has to be super heavy. Especially with us in it. She'd have to take out every piece of furniture and us, too. Even then . . ."

"She's definitely going to want to show him the house, though," Mac said. "She won't be able to resist. Magnus's house. Magnus made all the furniture. How clever Magnus was! What a genius! She hasn't had a chance to brag to anyone but us, at least not for a long time."

Lulu was hugging Pippy and looking from one of us to the other.

"You know what?" I said. "I bet she takes *us* out and puts us somewhere and leaves everything else."

Tanya drummed her fingers on the arm of the couch. "We have to do something clever. We could leave a note in the middle of the floor where the guy would be sure to see it."

"But she'd see it, too."

Tanya nodded and turned to Mac. "You're the writer. Pretend this is a book and you have to find a solution. I guess you're good with books."

"There isn't always a solution," Mac said seriously. "But there can be a possibility."

And in the end, he was the one who thought up the possibility. But I would be the one who'd have to make it work. Or not.

She discovered the leak when she brought our breakfast the next morning. We heard her heels tapping down the steps. There was a moment's pause, then more clicking as she walked over to where I knew the pipe jutted from the wall.

She came across to the dollhouse, lifted the roof, handed in our food.

Instead of "Good morning, Lambkins," she said, "Lambkins! We have a problem. I'll have to get a plumber down here. And I'm afraid that's going to disturb all of you. I'll need to go right now and call him." She sounded flustered, uncertain. That was the first time I'd seen her confused, and I gave Tanya a secret thumbs-up. Her confusion was a good sign.

Breakfast was a large pancake, cut in pieces and drenched with syrup. But the only two who ate and seemed to enjoy it were Lulu and Pippy.

Tanya pushed away her plate of untouched food

and leaned across the table, eyes bright with excitement. "When, Kyle?"

"Right now. We'll have to take a chance that she won't see it too soon."

They followed me into the bedroom.

I chose one of the brand-new oil paints, Scarlet Lake Red, and picked the thickest of the brushes. Tanya carried the palette and the linseed oil with us as we went back into the living room.

They all watched as I squeezed the fat rope of paint from the tube and swirled it and the oil around on the palette with the plastic stick. The paint was thick and smooth. I smelled the heady, sharp smell. A quick memory came with it. Art lessons in the gallery. The easels jumbled around. Richard in the old white shirt smeared with colors that he wore over his sweater every day, that hung empty on the coatrack when he went home at night.

Mac had moved the coffee table close, and I climbed on it so I could reach the top of the wall underneath where she always stood to reach in for us. The wall that was out of her direct view.

Tanya filled the brush with paint and gave it to me.

My hand was steady as I printed in giant letters.

HELP.

MRS. SHEPHERD KIDNAPPED US. WE ARE HIDDEN IN HER HOUSE.

It took a lot of paint refills. I emptied one tube, and Mac brought me a bright Viridian Green, which I squeezed onto the other side of the palette.

MCNAMARA CHANG

TANYA ROBERTS

LUPE SANCHEZ

KYLE WILSON

"What about John?" Tanya asked quietly

She handed me a full dip of Lamp Black and I printed JOHN PONDERELLI and after it, smaller, (DECEASED).

"Okay?" I asked, wiping my hands on a rag that looked like one of Victor's T-shirts.

"Thanks." I saw tears in Tanya's eyes.

"You didn't put Pippy, you didn't put Pippy," Lulu wailed, so I got up again and added the little dog's name to the list. On Lulu's orders, I put a CH for champion in front of it. "Pippy needs her full title," she told me.

I stood looking at the names and I thought, *The plumber won't see these. If he does, he won't believe it.*

But we were desperate. What did we have to lose?

Tanya wrinkled her nose. "It smells all painty in here. We need to open a few windows . . . joke, joke, joke," she said. And then her eyes widened. "Kyle! She's going to smell this the minute she lifts the roof. Oh, no! She'll start looking to see what we've been doing."

"Somebody come up with something, quick," I begged.

"Do you want me to do almost cartwheels again?" Lulu asked. "And say the lines?"

"No, sweetie." Tanya stroked Lulu's cheek. "I don't think that would work twice."

"I know," Mac said. "Help me carry out one of the canvases. The biggest one there is. Tanya, bring more brushes, more paint."

Lulu pouted. "I want to do something." I glanced at her baby face and realized that for her, this was a game and she was a part of it.

"You can bring some of the brushes," I said. "But we have to hurry."

We propped the big canvas on three chairs against the wall, opposite the one that held our message. The wall that would be directly in her line of vision if she stood where she always stood to lift off the roof. I hated these "ifs." They were scary, like the "somehows" Tanya and I were always running into. But we couldn't let them stop us.

Frantically I squeezed paint from the tubes, listening all the time for the telltale click of her heels on the stone steps. Burnt Umber, Vermilion, piling mounds of color on the palette. Lulu wanted to join in, and Tanya helped her. Even as they squelched out the paint, I'd started making lines and squares and squiggles on the canvas, an eye with a slit of a black pupil, a bird in the corner, anything to get the paint on there. Lots of it. And always listening.

"This was a really great idea, Mac," Tanya said. "You did well."

I glanced sideways and saw her touch Mac's arm. Then she added, breathlessly, "Everybody act normal. Here she comes."

"Don't stop, Kyle," Mac whispered. "You standing there, painting, will attract her attention more than anything else. She'll be looking at you. She'll be ecstatic."

Click, click, click. Those high-heeled shoes. Scarlet Lake Red or Lamp Black.

"Everybody! Be admiring Kyle's painting. Nobody look at the other wall," Mac whispered. "Do you understand, Lulu? Don't look at the wall with your name on it."

Lulu nodded and put her thumb in her mouth.

I slipped my hand in my pocket and rubbed John's stone. *Are you with us, John? Are you watching over us?*

Tanya held Lulu. Mac and I stood with our shoulders touching as we waited in silence for the roof to lift.

CHAPTER 16

"Oh, my, Kyle! You're painting again. And it looks so interesting!"

Blood pounded in my ears as the Shepherd leaned forward above the living room for a better look. What if she leaned farther in, looked down, and saw the words on the wall? But she didn't.

"I'm so sorry to interrupt," she said. "But the plumber is coming right away and I do have to move you. You *will* be able to get your inspiration back, won't you, Kyle?"

I nodded. "Definitely."

She lifted me first, the big gloved hand closing firmly around me, lifting me so quickly my stomach dropped out. I'd had plenty of her lifting by now, but I could never get used to it.

She clippity-clopped up the steps and into her house.

"Here we are," she said. "And I promise you won't be in here long."

I had a glimpse of a big, polished wooden box with a domed lid that was slatted like a venetian blind. She lifted the lid and set me on the floor inside. The lid came down, a key turned, and I was in striped dark and light.

There was enough room for me to pace eighteen steps in length, fourteen in width. I took a running jump, felt my ankle give a little as I reached for the slats above me. I was way short.

She brought Mac next. I heard him ask her, "Are you looking forward to showing the plumber the dollhouse?"

"Yes, McNamara," she said. "It will be a treat for both of us. His name is Mr. Cooper. He seemed very affable on the phone."

"He'll be interested in how cleverly Dr. Shepherd did the house plumbing," Mac told her. "He'll appreciate it."

Smart, Mac, I thought. *Good move.*

Then he was in beside me. The lid closed, the key

turned in the lock. "At least it's bigger than John's coffin," he muttered.

"Boost me up," I said. "I know it's locked, but let's see if we can at least reach it. If we could only break one of those slats."

I stood on his shoulders and tried to insert my fingers through one of the long, narrow openings, to get a handhold, but the spaces between were too small, even for a hand the size of mine. "We'll think of a way," I said. "It would be better if we could get out, the four of us, and hide. In case the plumber doesn't see our message. Even if he does, better we're hidden somewhere till help comes. Safer."

"Safer," Mac repeated.

We both understood the risks if the Shepherd knew she'd been discovered. First she'd get rid of the evidence. And we'd be the kind of evidence it wouldn't be hard to get rid of. I shivered.

"Slide down," Mac whispered. "She's coming back."

Tanya was lifted in next, holding Lulu, holding Pippy.

Each time the lid lifted, the chest flooded with light. I saw a ceiling with a fan and an old-fashioned lamp fixture with three pink glass tulips. It could be her bedroom. I'd missed it when she'd given me her house tour.

The lid closed for the third and probably last time. The key turned again in the lock.

"I don't want to be in here," Lulu wailed.

Tanya said, "Shh, now. I'm here."

The Shepherd's voice came from above, close to the lid. There was an added darkness in the box as her shadow leaned across it. "If Mr. Cooper takes longer than he thinks, I'll bring you snacks and drinks."

We didn't hear her go, her footsteps muffled by the rug.

"Just pray Mr. Cooper has sharp eyes and a quick brain," Tanya said.

"Why won't she let us out?" Lulu whimpered. "Please, Mrs. Shepherd! Don't leave us!"

"She's gone for now, sweetie," Tanya comforted. "But she'll be back."

"It's scary in here." Lulu sobbed.

"No, it's not. Not really. See the way we're all striped? Like zebras. Have you ever seen a zebra, Lulu?" Tanya's soothing voice went on and on.

The rest of us said nothing. Maybe we were all silently praying for Mr. Cooper's sharp eyes and quick brain.

"Let's move so we're together in a circle and hold hands," I said. And then I added, "Pippy, too. We can hold his paw, okay, Lulu?"

"Do you think she'll show him the house before or after he fixes the pipe?" Tanya asked me.

"After," Mac and I said together.

"Will he see the words, Kyle? Please tell me he'll see them. If he doesn't—"

"He will," I said. "He can't miss them."

But will she see it first? I thought but didn't say. *Will she think of some clever explanation? Or somehow be able to hide it from him?* And there was still that awful question—would he take it seriously or just laugh it off?

In the closed space I could hear the others breathing.

"Lulu? Would you like me to sing to you?" Tanya asked then.

"Yes." Such a small voice. "The love song. And take me in your lap."

"Sure." Tanya pulled Lulu against her and began to sing, so softly it was almost a whisper.

> *"What the world needs now*
> *Is love, sweet love."*

Pippy lay down beside me, and I stroked her warm head. Poor little Pippy, caught in this trap like the rest of us. I wondered how small she'd be in ordinary human eyes. Big as a mouse, maybe. Big as a puppy biscuit, with legs.

Tanya had said she wasn't much of a singer, and she was right. But the words were good. I'd never listened to the words of this song before, and I decided they were really wise. But there were all kinds of love, weren't there? The kind my mother had for me and I had for her. Real love, and the sick kind Mrs. Shepherd had for us.

When Tanya finished singing, that awful, frightened silence came down again.

"We're going to go home soon," I said as if I were really sure. "Let's each say what we're going to do when we're out of here."

"First a shower with hot, hot water," Mac said.

"Don't get pulled down the drain," Tanya told him.

"Oh, that's true. Maybe I'll wait for that shower till I've grown back to normal size. Okay then. First off, I'll get me a triple-size burger and a double order of fries."

"And then you'll finish the book," I said.

"I'll finish this book and the next one." I felt him move a little. "It's like a memorial to my mother. Not too many people know the old Irish epics. They are miraculous, filled with violence and beauty. The names take your breath away. Finnabair, Cormac Connlongas in his dark gray cloak and red embroidered tunic, the exiled sons of Uisliu." He seemed to be looking past us to a time and a place we didn't know. He shook his head, smiled. "Yes. When I get out of here, I will write. If I play baseball, that will be my hobby, not the other way around. There's something about going through the valley like this—"

"What's a valley?" Lulu asked. "Did I go through it?"

"It means going through a bad place, a bad time," Tanya said. "And we all did that."

I liked it that she spoke in the past tense. As if the bad times were over.

"Anyway," Mac finished. "Your turn, Tanya."

"Ditto on the burger and fries," she said.

"But first we're going to go kite flying, right, Tanya?" Lulu's voice was reproachful. "You said we'd do that first."

"And we will. It will be a breezy day, filled with

clouds and sunshine. A true kite flying day."

We sat, each one of us probably picturing a day like that, longing for it. Tanya broke the silence. "And then we'll go for those burgers and fries." She leaned down and kissed the top of Lulu's head.

"And after that?" I asked quietly.

"Will I have my violin back?"

"You will." I gave her hand a squeeze and thought I felt her fingers curl around mine for an instant. But I wasn't sure.

"It's a really cool violin, the tone, the depth. It belonged to my mother. She could play like a dream. It was the only thing she left me. I carried it with me through three foster homes." She was quiet for a minute. "The Shepherd told me there were scholarships to Juilliard." She stopped to explain to Lulu. "Juilliard's a famous music school. Where you can learn to be really good."

Lulu nodded. "Like the place John was going to, the one to make him sing even better."

"Like that," Tanya agreed. "The Shepherd said she had influence. She could get me in. She said she could tell, just by listening to me play, that I had 'undisclosed talent.' Her words."

"I bet you could get in without influence," Mac said, and I wished I had said it first.

"I'm going to try by myself, in a couple of years." Tanya's voice got dreamy. "Did you know the students at Juilliard have their own orchestra? Sometimes they have recitals. They were in Lincoln Center in New York at the John Adams festival last spring. Billy Lee told me about it."

"Billy Lee?" I asked.

"Another musical freak I met in Santa Cruz. I was so stupid," she went on. "When the Shepherd told me about all her influential connections, I would have gone with her anywhere."

"You'll make it, Tanya," I muttered. This time I said it first. "And another thing. When this is over, and we're out of here, we'll be famous. Did you ever think of that? Mac, you'll have such a story to tell, every publisher in the business will be fighting to get ahold of your books. They'll want the ones you wrote here and the ones you'll do next."

"Cool!" Mac gave a snort of laughter.

"And Tanya, Juilliard will be begging for you." I held up a hand and moved it as if following newspaper print. "Young violin prodigy, kidnapped. Holds on to her violin through the entire ordeal!"

"Except I didn't," Tanya said. "The Shepherd did."

"But you never stopped playing it in your heart," I said softly, and this time I knew for sure her fingers curled around mine.

"Let's just get out first," she said shakily.

"And will I be Shirley Temple?" Lulu asked.

"No. You'll be Lupe Sanchez, beautiful child entertainer who dances like a dream. If you want to be," I added.

Lulu put her chin in her hands. "I might rather be one of those ladies who rides a horse in a circus, you know, with the shiny, spangly dress?"

"That's what you'll be, then," I told her.

"What about you, Kyle?" Mac stretched his long legs out as far as they would go and leaned over to touch his toes.

"Well, I'll be doing what I want to do. I'll be painting. Maybe I'll even get a scholarship myself to somewhere, later. You never know."

Tanya still held my hand.

And then Mac said, "Just think, if we hadn't had undisclosed talent, the Shepherd wouldn't have taken us . . . patron of the arts that she is."

"Oh, man!" Tanya sighed. "The good and the bad."

"And the ugly," I added.

"I think I'll hug my mama first, though," Lulu announced. "Even before the kite day. I'll hug her and hug her and hug her."

We didn't seem to have anything else to say. The talking had been good, the little uplifts of optimism. But we were here, locked up, and everything, our freedom, our lives, depended on Mr. Cooper. Fear surged through me, drying my mouth. My ankle ached, and I wished I had some more of those baby aspirin.

Mac sneezed. And sneezed again. "It's dusty in here. Or smelly. There's not enough air."

"Don't say that," Tanya warned. "There's plenty of air." I heard her take a small, gaspy breath.

"Nobody panic," I said. "We'll be out of here soon."

And right then, from somewhere far, far away, I heard the faint chime of a doorbell.

"The plumber's here," Tanya breathed.

I jumped up. "Everybody yell," I said. "Yell!"

We screamed our loudest. Pippy barked and barked. My ears felt like bursting. But how far away was the Shepherd's front door? Too far for our puny voices?

We stopped and listened to the silence. Listened

for the sound of a man's heavy footsteps tramping into the Shepherd's bedroom, a rough, loud voice asking, "What's that? I thought I heard something. What's in that box?"

But there was no sound anywhere.

CHAPTER 17

"But he hasn't been to the dollhouse yet. He hasn't seen the wall," Tanya said at last. "That's our trump card, and we haven't played it yet."

The echoes of our shouts and yells, of Pippy's barks, still filled the closed-up space.

"Let's not sit and wait for that," I said.

Tanya's voice was quiet. "You mean, in case it doesn't happen?"

I pretended I didn't hear.

"I know you tried to break the lid and couldn't," she said. "But my fingers are smaller. I might get them through the slats."

She stood on Mac's shoulders, and I heard the

scratch of her nails on the wood, a gasp, and then her voice, small and weak. "Pull! Everybody pull on my legs."

Maybe half a minute later she panted, "Okay. That's enough. I'm not doing any good."

I helped her down.

Standing next to her, I saw that she had made loose fists of her hands.

"Let me see," I said, taking one of them and prying open the fingers.

She tried to pull away. "It's nothing."

I eased her fist open. Blood oozed around three of her nails. I glanced at her, lifted the other hand. One nail had pulled away from the skin, the edges ragged and leaking blood.

"Oh, Tanya," I whispered.

"They're okay. They don't hurt that much." Her mouth was set in a tight line.

"They hurt," I said.

Lulu began to sob and said, "Tanya. Oh, Tanya. Let me see."

"It's nothing," Tanya said.

We slumped down on the floor of the chest.

We were here, and we weren't getting out. Not yet. Not till, and unless, Mr. Cooper came to save us.

We didn't talk much after that, just sat in our circle of slanting light, listening.

"I wonder what he's doing now?" Tanya asked. I noticed her once surreptitiously sucking on the ends of her fingers.

"He's turned off the water," Mac said. "He's replacing the broken part of the pipe. He's putting on the water again to make sure there are no leaks."

We sat for a few more minutes in the terrible silence, listening.

Time passed.

It felt like a lot of time.

"Mrs. Shepherd didn't bring us snacks," Lulu whimpered.

"Do you think she's forgotten we're in here?"

"Shh, sweetheart," Tanya whispered. "She hasn't forgotten."

Every now and then, one of us got up and stretched and paced.

And listened.

Pippy made three small puddles in one corner. "It's all right," we told her.

"Maybe he found the message and said he was going to the cops, and she whacked him over the head with that old piece of pipe," Tanya said. "I wouldn't put it past her."

"Maybe she liked him a lot and she's giving him lemonade and cookies," Lulu said. "Our snacks."

I shook my head. "Naw! Hey, Lulu? Want to play pat-a-cake?"

"Uh-uh," Lulu said. "Not now."

I realized I was having trouble breathing. I reminded myself that there was plenty of air coming through. I wouldn't let myself imagine that the box was getting smaller. I got up and did some running in place, ran till I felt sweat chill on my skin. When I sat down, my stretched-out legs were touching Tanya's. They didn't have to. I could have moved, but I didn't.

"Lulu's asleep," Tanya whispered.

"Good." I was thinking out loud. "Why on earth did the Shepherd take a little kid like Lulu anyway? Lulu doesn't fit in with her pattern."

"She told Lulu she'd always wanted a sweet little girl," Mac said wearily. "She couldn't resist."

We sagged against one another, too worn out to sit straight.

"The dog was her bait," Mac went on. "That, and

a balloon. She left Pippy in her car, at the L.A. county fair, and she asked Lulu if she'd like to have a nice balloon and come meet her little dog. Lulu went like a lamb to the slaughter. A Lambkin."

Tanya smoothed Lulu's curls with the flat of her hand, and Lulu gave a sleepy moan.

I pounded my fist on the floor. "Why didn't the Shepherd get caught? Why?"

"Well, she was clever," Mac said. "She changed her locales. Nobody would ever suspect such a nice lady. Why would they? What would be her motive?"

"And of course, there were no dead bodies," Tanya said. "With teenagers, there's always the suspicion that they just ran away. And with me, that suspicion was a true fact. I bet they searched really hard for Lulu."

"Why—?" I began, and then we heard the bedroom door open.

"Yell! Yell again! It has to be him." I scrambled up, and we all began screaming.

"Help! Help! Mr. Cooper! We're in here. In the box!"

Lulu wakened and screamed with us in terror and confusion.

But then, outside the box, the growl began, low

as a grumble, rising, rising. It could have been some wild, hungry animal out there. But we knew it was something worse.

I jammed my hands against my ears. Pippy yelped. Lulu's screams turned to shrieks.

We'd failed.

She was here.

For a minute there was a frightening silence. Then she began to shake the box. We were tossed from side to side, like sailors in a storm, this way, that way, staggering against one another, piling up in one corner.

The key clicked in the lock.

The lid opened, and we scrambled up and stood there, blinking into the dazzle of light.

She leaned over, looking down at us, her face rigid with rage. She was so close I could see the pocks in her skin where once she had had zits. I could see the white roots of her red hair. I could see the shiny green stuff on her eyelids.

"You could have gotten me into real trouble this time." Her voice wavered with fury. "How dare you! How dare you!" She took a breath, maybe to calm herself. It didn't calm me.

When she spoke again her voice was deadly

quiet. "Fortunately, I decided to place Betsy and Britney and Victor and Brian in the house before I showed it to Mr. Cooper. My *good* doll children. Imagine my horror when I saw what you'd done. I presume this scenario was your idea, Kyle?"

"It was all of us," Mac said.

"You were in this, too, McNamara? After everything I've done for you. How sharper than a serpent's tooth it is to have a thankless child."

"Mrs.—Mrs. Shepherd?" Lulu's sobs had changed into pitiful gulps. "Please, Mrs. Shepherd, can we go back now? It's bad here."

"No," the Shepherd said. "This time you've all gone too far. I wasn't even able to show Mr. Cooper Magnus's wonderful house. You deprived me of that. You deprived Magnus of the praise he so deserves."

"Get over it," Tanya said. "Magnus is dead. D—E—A—D, dead."

The Shepherd took a jerky step back.

I spoke quickly before she could react further. "I know you're mad at us. But Lulu didn't do anything. She's scared and hungry."

"I'm sorry you're hungry, Lulu. I'll bring some food. As for the rest of you—" Her green-lidded eyes were flat as a cobra's. "You are too difficult. I've decided to exchange you."

"Exchange us?" I almost stopped breathing. "You mean, let us go and get four, I mean three, other— uh, children? Or just be content with your dolls?"

"You understand very well what I mean. I can't let you go, Kyle. You know that, too. Fortunately for me, but unfortunately for you, an exchange of new children will only be a small problem." The venom in her smile matched her snake eyes.

The lid of the box banged down, the key grated, and we stood again in light and shadow.

"Exchange?" Tanya said. "Exchange?"

We didn't look at one another.

"We'll be okay," I said automatically. But in my heart I knew this was the end for us. I remembered the Shepherd's eyes, the finality in her voice. She was crazy, and it would be nothing to her to carry that craziness another step forward.

I felt in my pocket for John's angel, rubbing it between my finger and thumb. It gave me comfort, the way it had done since the beginning. I'd been selfish with it. I'd give it to Tanya. It might comfort her now when we most needed it.

"Look!" I held it out on the palm of my hand.

"What is it?" Tanya didn't even glance at me.

"John's stone. I found it in the pocket of the khakis he wore, way back."

She set Lulu down. "It was John's?" Her bloodied fingers touched it gently. "John's? Why didn't you give it to me before?"

She was looking at me in amazement, and I had no reason to give her.

"I don't know. There's something scratched on it. You can't see it in this light." I was babbling, trying to get the words out, not wanting to meet her eyes. "The scratching has the shape of an angel. It was like a message, a sort of blessing from someone I didn't even know. From John. I've kept it with me every day. I knew you'd want it, Tanya, and I couldn't bear to give it up." I shrugged. "Maybe it is only a meaningless scratching on there, but to me it was always my angel."

I'd thought Lulu was already asleep, but she wasn't. "Kyle didn't want you to be sad all over again, Tanya," she said. "That's why he didn't give you the stone."

"I would have wanted to have it," Tanya said.

"Something of John's. He was the best friend I ever had."

Then Mac said, "Can I see it?"

Tanya gave it to him.

He took it, holding it up to a shaft of light, and all at once I had such a dazzle of thought that it took my breath away. It could work. I sat down on the floor of the box, boneless, my heart thundering inside me.

"You're going to save us, Mac," I said at last. "McNamara Chang and John's angel."

CHAPTER 18

"Mac," I said. "Wrap your hand around the stone. Feel it."

"Okay." He rolled it between his fingers. "But I have no idea what you're talking about."

I took a deep breath. "How does it feel? It's round. It's smooth. It's hard. It fits perfectly in your hand. It feels familiar. What is it?"

"A baseball," he said. "Smaller, though. You wouldn't have as much control using a ball this small."

"You'd have enough."

Tanya was suddenly alert. "What is this? What are you thinking?"

"Mac," I asked, "do you remember the story of

David and the giant, Goliath? How David killed him with a stone?"

Slowly Mac nodded, and all the time the stone tumbled and wove, over and across his fingers.

"David had a slingshot, if I remember right," Tanya said breathlessly.

"I know. But we have a star pitcher. How fast was your fastball, Mac?"

"Ninety miles an hour. On a good day," Mac said.

"This better be a perfect day," I told him. "Look, when she comes back, when she opens the lid, her head is going to be so close to us, closer than she's ever been. She won't be as far away as home plate, Mac. Not as far as the catcher's mitt. Mac! You can do it. You can pitch this stone, this baseball, right in the middle of her forehead. Hard and straight. Ninety miles an hour."

"But it's so *small*," Mac said.

I nodded. "A bullet's small, too."

"Oh, my gosh!" Tanya closed her eyes. "It might work. It could."

"I haven't pitched in months," Mac said nervously.

"It's like riding a bicycle," I told him. "You never forget how."

I felt confident. I felt sure.

The tension and excitement had brought Lulu wide awake.

"Are you going to hurt Mrs. Shepherd?" she asked. "Don't hurt her."

"Just enough so we can get away," I said. No need to tell Lulu that to get away we'd have to hurt the Shepherd bad.

"Is that okay with you, LuluBelle? Is it cool?"

Lulu nodded.

"Wait a second." Tanya held up her hand. The shaft of light left her face half in shadow. "Why can't Mac just pitch the stone up at the slats and try to break them? If he could punch a hole, we could squeeze through and get out."

"I could try pitching through the space," Mac said. "But suppose the stone goes through without making a hole? Then it's gone forever. And we're still in here."

Tanya bit her lip. "That's true."

"Besides, she could come while we're trying to get away and scoop us back. The way she did with me," I said.

We looked at one another in silence.

"Better that she be out of commission," Mac said.

"Agreed?" I asked Tanya.

"Agreed."

I paused. "Lulu?"

Lulu frowned her baby frown. "It's whatever Tanya says," she told me. "Tanya knows."

"Okay." I was filled with confidence. "This will work, Mac. I feel it. I'll warm you up. Tanya and Lulu and Pippy, you should go in a corner and stay safe. I'm going to catch the ball for Mac."

He threw some soft pitches.

"No good," I told him. "Harder, Mac."

"You don't have a mitt. If I throw harder, I could break your knuckles."

"Harder," I said. "Practice time is short, Mac. She could come back at any minute."

Mac took a couple more steps back. "There's not much room."

"That's all you've got," I said.

My hands were on fire, tingling, blazing with pain. I shook them from the wrist.

"Here." Tanya pushed me aside. "Mac! Give me a turn! Pitch to me!"

"But your fingers are already—"

"Throw to me," she said.

Lulu jumped up and down. "Me, too, Mac," but I

pulled her over into the corner beside me. "Not this time, sweetie. Come sit with me."

"Do your hands hurt a lot, Kyle?" she asked. "I'll blow on them."

She lifted one of my hands and blew her sweet little hot breath on them. Over her head, I watched Mac and Tanya, throwing, catching. I could tell Tanya was hurting. She was dropping the stone more than she was catching it. But always she returned it to Mac for another pitch.

"Did you like me blowing on your hands?" Lulu asked.

"It helped a lot," I said.

"Do you want Pippy to lick them?"

"Okay." I held out my palms for Pippy's wet, soothing tongue.

"That was so good," I told Lulu. "I bet Tanya would like Pippy to lick hers, too."

Mac stood now, head bent, not throwing any-more.

"What's up?" I asked nervously.

"Just thinking about it. I'll be pitching up this time," he said.

"This won't be your usual strike zone either, Mac. Today the strike zone is here." I touched my finger to a spot between my eyes. "Your hardest ever, Mac. But it has to be a beanball, absolutely on target. This may be our last best chance."

"I know."

"Should I massage your arm?" I asked, but he shook his head.

"She'll be here pretty soon," I muttered.

We sat again in the circle, to wait. How much waiting had we done over these past months? How much hoping?

Lulu brought Pippy to Tanya.

"It works," I told her. "Lick therapy."

Minutes ticked by. I tried not to keep looking at my watch. Wasn't she going to come? She had to come sometime.

"It seems to me that using John's stone is a kind of justice," Tanya said after a long silence. "He would have liked that."

Mac tossed the stone back and forth between his hands and sat staring at his feet.

"I wish she'd hurry," Tanya said.

"I hear her," I said. "Are you ready, Mac?"

He stood. "Ready."

She swung the lid back on its hinges. It was suddenly bright, a clear, steady brightness. Her face loomed. She had something in her hand that she bent to put in the box.

In front of me Mac went into his windup, bent his knees, curved his back in the familiar pitcher's arc—and hurled.

She made a surprised, stunned sound, like air coming out of a beach ball.

The bag of torn-up crackers she'd been holding dropped with a small thud into the box.

She disappeared from view.

The lid of the box hung open.

"Quick," I said. "Mac. Boost me up."

I stood on his shoulders and eased my head over the box rim.

She lay there on the carpet, on her back, moaning softly. Blood trickled from her forehead. I saw the neat, dark red wound between her eyes.

Seeing it I felt dazed and almost sick.

I swiveled and looked down at their upturned faces.

"Bull's-eye," I said.

CHAPTER 19

We helped one another scramble out of the box and down the other side, onto the rug where the Shepherd lay.

I found the stone, wiped the blood from it, and slid it back in my pocket. Tanya was watching me. I took out the stone again and held it toward her, but she shook her head. "I don't need it," she said. "It's yours."

"We'll share it," I said, and Tanya smiled.

Lulu stood, staring down at the Shepherd. "Is she dead? Like John?"

"No," Tanya told her. "She's just hurt, and she's sleeping."

I glanced up at Mac. "Good job, man. Right on

the money." Then I added. "We've got to tie her up as fast as we can and get out of here."

We dragged a sash off a bathrobe, found a belt and a pair of panty hose that lay on her chair. Together we bound her ankles and then her hands. It took all three of us to cinch the belt buckle and make the knots tight, standing on her stomach, swarming all over her.

She never moved.

I checked her huge wrist for a pulse and found one, banging away like a drum.

"She's okay," I told the others. "Come on, get moving."

What if she could break through our knots and grab us again? I tried to think through the panic.

"Should we gag her?" Tanya asked.

"I'd be scared to chance it," I said. "Besides, there's nobody to hear even if she did yell." I glanced around. "Everybody check for a phone."

There wasn't one in the bedroom. There was a painting, though. *My painting!*

I stood, numb with shock. The Shepherd had bought it. She'd hung it in her house. And I'd stupidly thought someone had seen it there in the window of the gallery and loved it and wanted it. That wasn't why the Shepherd had bought it. It had been a part of her plot. Maybe she thought it would make me feel welcome. Something nasty and bitter rose in my throat.

I knew we had to go. I knew I had to leave my painting hanging there in her creepy house. I vowed I'd come back and get it someday. The Shepherd didn't deserve to have it.

I took one last look at it as we ran in a straggle through the open door and along the hallway. We were getting away!

I had an almost surreal feeling as we rushed down the polished hallway, slipping and skidding on the floor I'd slipped and skidded on as I tried to escape that first terrible night.

In the dining room we slowed. Mac put his hand on the thick leg of the table, and for a moment we stared up at our smaller table on top of it, ready for Mrs. Shepherd's next guest. One of us. How long would that have gone on, week after week, till the end of our lives, or the end of hers? I felt myself shudder, and suddenly Tanya was beside me, her hand in mine. I remembered to only hold it gently.

She looked across to the corner where her violin leaned in its scuffed black case.

Tanya stopped to look at it.

I pulled on her arm. "Later, Tanya. We have to keep going."

"I'll come back for you," she called out to it.

"And I'll come back for my manuscripts," Mac said.

"And bring Old Bear for me, Mac. Promise?"

"Promise," Mac said.

I'd get my painting, too, I promised myself.

We were running again.

"Here's a phone," Mac called from the front hallway. "I don't think we can get to it, though. It's on a shelf, high on the wall."

The shelf was glass, supported only by two golden gargoyle heads.

"If we bring over a chair," Tanya began, then shook her head. "We'd still be miles from it."

"Damn," I said. "But we can run to the house at the end of the road. We won't have to go across the field." I smashed one of her brass ornaments through the long dining room window.

And we were free.

We ran down the long road, wheezing and panting, worn out already. Mac carried Lulu on his back. I carried Pippy when she sat down, refusing to go farther. I remembered Nellie, who'd done the same thing. We were always checking the road behind us, jittery as field mice. I could hardly breathe. My thoughts wheeled around the last time I had almost escaped, there in that overgrown meadow. I remembered the shears, shining sharp in the sun, the butterfly net. When some creature, small as we were, rustled the long grass close to us, my nerves shrieked. Was she coming after us? But all was quiet. I thought of my mother. I imagined her face when she saw me again. But I'd be so small, so infinitesimal. How would she handle that? I'd say, quickly, "This isn't going to last, Mom. I'll be back to normal really soon." I tried to stay calm.

It was evening, the sun sliding behind the trees, the house ahead of us. There were still no lights inside it, but there was a friendliness to it, a wel-coming, a homeliness. We stopped on the grass outside its white wooden gate. A small bike leaned against the front steps. A swing hung from a reaching oak tree.

"It makes me want to cry, it's so normal," Tanya whimpered. The gate was fastened, the latch high. Mac climbed the rail, hand over hand, but it was still too far above his head.

We hammered on the wood with our fists. "C'mon! C'mon, help us somebody!"

"What if they have a big, big dog?" Lulu asked nervously.

"If they had, it would be barking by now," I told her. I hoped I was right.

"Oh, my gosh!" a small voice behind us said. "Oh, my gosh! Tiny people!"

We swung around.

A little girl, probably Lulu's age, in overalls and a blue T-shirt, stood gaping at us. She was pulling a red wagon that had toy trucks and tractors in it. Her hands and the knees of her overalls were clumped with dirt.

She came closer, head to one side, and walked around us twice. "Who are you guys? Are you real?" She came even closer. "Are you aliens?"

"No," I said. "Can you open the gate for us? We need help."

"Oh, look at the little dog." She put her hand out to Pippy, and Pippy gave a tired, warning growl.

Mac stood as if on guard, looking back the way we'd come.

"No sign of her?" I asked.

"Not so far," he said.

"Are your parents in the house?" I asked the little girl.

"Sure." She reached up and unlatched the gate. "Come on in." We began to limp toward the path. "Are you tired?" she asked. "I'll give you a ride." Without another word, she lifted each of us, effortlessly, and put us in the red wagon to jostle there with her trucks and tractors.

She stopped at the bottom of the steps and called loudly, "Mom! Dad! Come and see what I found." She beamed down at us.

"Do you know Shirley Temple?" Lulu asked.

We sat together in a faded flowered easy chair, waiting for the police to come. I knew, when they did, it would be hard for them to believe their senses. We'd be explaining and answering questions for a long time. Our lives would be forever changed.

And what about the Shepherd? I could only guess.

I felt in my pocket for John's stone and thought of the angel, flying away from us, flying upward from earth to heaven. "Thank you," I whispered. "You can go home now.

"We can all go home."

Other compelling novels by Eve Bunting

The Summer of Riley
Pb 0-06-440927-9
Lb 0-06-029142-7

Blackwater
Pb 0-06-440890-6

The In-Between Days
Pb 0-06-440563-X

Is Anybody There?
Pb 0-06-440347-5

Nasty, Stinky Sneakers
Pb 0-06-440507-9

Our Sixth-Grade Sugar Babies
Pb 0-06-440390-4

Joanna Cotler Books
An Imprint of HarperCollinsPublishers

www.harpercollinschildrens.com